# PRAISE FOR

## THE SOUND OF VIOLET

### "Entertaining, well-paced, and highly visual."

"Wolf, an award-winning filmmaker, has adapted this first novel from his own original screenplay, and its cinematic potential clearly shows. The high-concept narrative is entertaining, well-paced, and highly visual. It's a charming, humorous, and hopeful tale. A quirky, touching love story that offers insights into autism, religion, and personal tragedy."

*- Kirkus Reviews*

### "A wonderfully well-written, funny, romantic love story."

"Unique and inspirational. *The Sound of Violet* is not your average romance. Rarely do I find myself so captivated by a book that I cannot put it down for nearly two hours. Pick up this book and get lost in the beauty of their relationship. My only complaint would be that the story had an ending, as all stories do, and I did so want to keep reading on. Most highly recommended. *The Sound of Violet* is simply remarkable."

*- Readers' Favorite*

### "A sweet and entertaining romantic comedy."

"By turning conventions of contemporary romance on its stilettos and swapping out the typical sassy, fashion-obsessed female protagonist for an autistic male who reads jokes from index cards, Wolf puts a fresh spin on the genre. Adapted from his award-winning screenplay, *The Sound of Violet* shows signs of its origins with snappy dialogue and humorous, well-staged scenes. A sweet and entertaining romantic comedy, *The Sound of Violet* touches on autism and the power of faith. It will appeal to any reader who enjoys a blend of quirky characters, humor and drama."

*- Blue Ink Review*

# "Heartfelt, out-of-the-ordinary romance."

"A romantic twentysomething fails to spot that his new girlfriend is a prostitute because he is autistic. The situation has ample comedic potential, but it isn't just played for laughs. This warm, witty story does not shy away from serious themes like exploitation, redemption, and true love. *The Sound of Violet* explores heavy issues with a light touch. It's easy to see this being adapted into an enjoyable movie."

— *Foreword Reviews*

# "*The Sound of Violet* is simply remarkable."

"Mr. Wolf's novel is beautifully written. Rarely will I find myself captivated by a book that I cannot put it down for nearly two hours. I read this book from start to finish in one sitting. Shawn was so sweet, and Mr. Wolf really strove to write him as believable as possible. My heart went out to his gentle nature and simple desire to be loved. After all, isn't that what we all want in life? Violet was a very sympathetic character and I found myself hoping more than anything for a happy ending for the pair. Pick up this book and get lost in the beauty of their relationship. *The Sound of Violet* is simply remarkable and was a complete pleasure to review."

— *Eclectic Ramblings*

# "Hilarious and Inventive."

"Love is one of the most powerful and mysterious forces in the world. In *The Sound of Violet*, Allen Wolf explores the depth of this binding force in hilarious and inventive ways and makes us think about what it is that brings two unlikely people together."

— *Tom Zoellner, Winner of The National Book Critics Circle Award*

# "Wolf creates a gripping and heartwarming read out of the most surprising relationship."

"*The Sound of Violet* was a novel I really wanted to savor and appreciate. It did not disappoint, in fact, it outdid my expectations. It was a really heartwarming story and dealt with the two worlds of Shawn and Violet colliding well. The characters in this novel are fleshed out well, especially with their detailed backstories that make them feel like real people. I almost didn't want the story to come to an end but knew it had to."

*- Reedsy Discovery Reviews*

# "A modern love story that will leave readers glued to the pages."

"*The Sound of Violet* is a modern love story that will leave readers glued to the pages as they wait for this addictive storyline to unfold. With plenty of humorous, light-hearted moments to balance out the underlying serious nature of the book, *The Sound of Violet* validates how the human experience is rooted in craving connection and understanding. In this unexpected love story, readers will ride the rollercoaster of emotions with the characters as they overcome challenges in life and love."

*- The Book Review Directory*

# AWARDS FOR

# THE SOUND
# OF VIOLET

Book of the Year Award, Foreword Reviews

Book of the Year Award, The Independent Author Network

Gold Medal Winner, Literary Classic Awards

Gold Medal Winner, Reader's Favorite Awards

Silver Medal Winner, Benjamin Franklin Awards

Bronze Medal, IP Awards

Finalist, USA News Book Awards

# THE SOUND OF VIOLET

## ALLEN WOLF

**MORNING STAR**
PUBLISHING

**The Sound of Violet**
Written by Allen Wolf
Kindly direct inquiries about the novel to:
info@morningstarpictures.com

AllenWolf.com
MorningStar-Publishing.com
TheSoundOfViolet.com

ISBN 978-1952844140

For my wife Ramesh

For those caught in human trafficking.
May you find freedom, hope, and grace.

# CONTENTS

Author's Note     i

Acknowledgments     ii

1   It's Stormy     1
2   Picky About the Guests     8
3   Pimps and Hos     16
4   The Girlfriend Experience     25
5   Auditions     32
6   Weird Place to Meet     40
7   Key Someone Else     51
8   A Different Wavelength     59
9   Everybody Lies     67
10   Her World     75
11   As Long as They Have Muffins     86
12   Something Unexpected     93
13   The Total Package     102
14   When Colors Sound Right     111
15   Let Her Go     120
16   Damaged Goods     129
17   A Price Tag on Her     138
18   You Have to Leave Now     147
19   A Big Mistake     157
20   I Know the Future     165
21   A Rare Talent     175
22   Colors and Sounds     186
    Make a Difference     195
    About Allen Wolf     196
    Movie Stills from *The Sound of Violet*     197
    Behind the Scenes of *The Sound of Violet*     201
    Book Club Discussion Questions     205
    Movies from Allen Wolf     206
    Games from Allen Wolf     209

# AUTHOR'S NOTE

While the original story of *The Sound of Violet* takes place in New York City, I was inspired to set the movie version in Seattle. I cherish both cities, but I kept the world of the novel in New York City because I thought readers would appreciate having unique experiences between the book and the movie.

I hope you enjoy *The Sound of Violet*.

All the best,

Allen Wolf
Author, Filmmaker, Game Creator

AllenWolf.com
TheSoundOfViolet.com

# ACKNOWLEDGMENTS

I'm so grateful for all the amazing people, friends, and community who
have supported me throughout the process of
writing this novel and creating the movie.

I'm thankful for the editing expertise of Sheryl Madden.

I'm thankful to everyone who worked behind the scenes and all these
terrific people who helped make the filming of *The Sound of Violet* possible:

Jeff Babcock

Scot and Kelly Barton

Sherry Boroumand

Chris, Carrie, and Daniel Cavigioli

Stephanie and William Christopher

Eileen and Brown Councill

David and Lira Clark

Tom and Katie Eggemeier

Neil and Dana Gamblin

Len and Denise Hoffmann

Debbie Knight

Sam and Carol Konswa

Eric and Leigh Anne Lynch

Doug and Christy Metzler

Sam and Cindy Moser

John Napier

Conrad Pope

Russ Schlecht

Dan and Jeanette Stevens

Peter and Amanda Trautmann

Jim and Carol VanArtsdalen

Louis and Faith Vision

Al and Malinda Wolf

Ramesh Wolf

# CHAPTER 1

## IT'S STORMY

Shawn didn't feel like an adult because adults were married, and he struggled to get through a date. He was twenty-four years old and looked like a man, with his powder-blue eyes, a trim physique, and a handsome face on a well-shaped head crowned with light brown hair. But he had never quite gotten used to his long arms and legs. When he walked, it looked like Shawn was carefully stepping between raindrops, especially when he started noticing all the colors around him.

The bashful sun peeked out from behind a gray curtain of clouds, kissing the Manhattan skyscrapers. Perfect dating weather. Shawn accompanied his latest date along a path through the High Line, a park that snaked above 11th Avenue, formerly abandoned railroad tracks that were transformed into a popular park years ago.

Emily looked pleasant but unremarkable as she trudged along, towering over him. She glanced his way, but Shawn couldn't peer into her eyes or anyone's eyes for that matter. When he did, it felt like he was staring into the sun. He'd force himself to do it, though, since people got uneasy when he darted his eyes away. But Shawn couldn't keep looking for long. The connection felt too electric, like he had jammed his finger into a wall socket.

The trees around them swayed in the wind; their branches collided against each other, clanging like wind chimes on a blustery day. The melodic tones transfixed Shawn.

Emily cocked her head to the side. "Are you even listening?" she asked.

He wasn't.

She knocked on an invisible wall between them. "Hello?"

Shawn broke out of his trance. "Sorry. I get distracted sometimes. By all the colors." He looked up at her height. "You must be good at basketball."

Her eyes narrowed. This wasn't Shawn's first awkward comment of the night. "And you must be great at miniature golf."

Shawn kicked the ground. "Not really."

"You're gonna ask me how the weather is up here? I'll save you the trouble." She popped the cap off her bottle and splashed water on his face. "Stormy!"

Shawn stood there, water dripping off his face, his mouth hanging open. His stomach ached as Emily stomped off, shaking her head. *What did I do this time? Maybe she doesn't like basketball.* She disappeared into the crowd of people surging around him.

Shawn sat on a park bench and logged into his online dating profile. Time to set up his next date. This was definitely a numbers game.

Later that week, he met Anna at the High Line. She was in her thirties, lean and frail looking. Friendly, but needy. Pictures of cats covered her rainbow suspenders. Her profile emphasized her love for all things feline, and Shawn hoped there would be more to her. He was getting less picky. Shawn led her down the path.

"Whenever I look at a cat, I try not to think about how lazy it is," Shawn said.

Anna raised her eyebrows. "They aren't lazy. They like to sleep."

"For seventy percent of their lives. Male lions sleep twenty hours a day, so you can tell they're related." Shawn had many more cat facts up his sleeve, but this one didn't land the way he thought it would. He hoped she'd find the rest of them captivating, so all the preparation he did for this date wouldn't be a waste of time.

"Cats are more intelligent than most people I date," Anna said.

"Then, you're dating the wrong people." Shawn peered at her face. "You know, you look different from your profile picture."

She slipped her hands into her pockets. "Confession time. That's actually my sister. I get a lot more interest when I use her pic. We're pretty similar, though. She's just more photogenic."

"No, she's a lot prettier than you."

Anna shrank back. "Are you for real?"

"Very," Shawn said. "She's the one who got the looks in your family."

Shawn's thoughts often raced out of his mouth, unedited. He knew people had to get used to that, or they wouldn't stick around for long. Anna blinked a few times as if she didn't know what to say. She scoffed, shrugged her shoulders, then hurried down one of the stairways that led to the street below.

Shawn knew better than to run after her. That had never worked on his previous dates. He peered at the red petals of the snapdragons circling the tree trunk next to him. The petals shivered and hummed, sounding like sustained chords of a violin.

On the following Saturday afternoon, he met Lindsay at the High Line. She looked identical to her picture, and he was relieved. She was in her twenties, with delicate features and dark hair pulled back from the planes of her face.

Their conversation began with how their days were going (fine) and about the state of the world (worrisome). They progressed to how expensive it was to reside in New York City (shockingly so, though technically Shawn didn't pay anything to live here). Then, the conversation detoured to how people perceive colors. This was Shawn's opportunity to shine. He fought to keep his thoughts on track as he strolled down the path with her.

"The light receptors in our eyes transmit messages to our brains about what we're seeing. Newton first observed that the surface of what we see reflects some colors and absorbs the rest. So, our eyes only perceive the reflected colors." He forced himself to stop, a skill that usually led people to talk with him longer.

Lindsay leaned into him. "You're a walking Wikipedia."

Shawn beamed. The sunlight sparkled off the brook next to them as it bubbled down the path. He lost himself for a moment in the melodic stream of the water. Lindsay nudged him.

"You there?" she asked.

"Oh. Sorry about that." He searched for a new topic. "The other day, I read an article about how this place would've still been an abandoned railroad track if someone didn't have the imagination to make it this beautiful."

Lindsay flicked her hair back. "So true."

"When it opened, people called it a secret, magic garden in the sky."

He started walking with a spring in his step. Lindsey reached over and held his hand. Startled, he shook her off. She stepped back with widened eyes. Shawn looked down; his arms hung to his sides.

"I'm sorry." He paused. "Sometimes touching can be too intense for me."

Lindsay poked her tongue against her cheek. "Oh."

"You look like you swallowed a lemon."

"And your profile didn't say, 'don't touch me.'"

"It used to, but I didn't get a lot of replies."

Lindsay bit her upper lip. "Are you on the spectrum?"

Shawn hesitated, then nodded. Whenever he told someone about his autism, their reactions were a mysterious mixed bag. Mysterious because Shawn couldn't understand what they were thinking. Sometimes those dates didn't last long after he brought this information to light, even after he explained he was high functioning. His brother, Colin, thought Shawn should keep his autism a secret for as long as possible. Or at least until the second date. But whenever Shawn kept those details in the dark, his dates seemed confused by how he would react to the world around him.

Shawn looked past her at a tall woman with black curly hair and olive skin dressed in a flowing wedding dress, holding a bouquet of purple and pink roses. The bride intertwined her hands with her smiling groom, who kissed the top of her head as a photographer snapped pictures of them holding each other. Shawn took in the moment. This was special.

Lindsay checked her watch. "So…"

"We should grab some coffee," Shawn said.

"Not a coffee drinker, I'm afraid."

"I didn't notice that on your profile." Shawn swallowed.

"You know what? I should get going. Need to meet someone. Don't know how I let that slip my mind. Sorry to cut this short."

"They look like they won the lottery," Shawn said, pointing to the couple behind her.

"It was so nice meeting you."

"Should we go out again? I like how you smell like laundry detergent." He realized he shouldn't have mentioned her scent. His brother always reminded him to keep olfactory observations to himself.

"I'll call you, okay?" she said, stepping back from him while keeping up the mask of her smile.

"I'll wait for your call," Shawn said, confident that day was just around the corner.

Her plastered grin continued as she made her way down the path. As Shawn watched her leave, the colors around him roared back to life. Tree branches clanged. The water tinkled. Petals hummed. The evening sun dazzled brightly. Shawn shielded his eyes and hurried his way back home.

Shawn shared a large condo with his grandmother on the Upper West Side of Manhattan, where the kitchen, dining room, and living room all enjoyed inspiring views of Central Park. Black and white oil paintings of scenes from the city—wet seals basking in the sun at the Central Park Zoo, the triangular Flatiron building dominating its street corner, a couple caught in intimate conversation in front of a boxy florist shop in SoHo—hung on the silver-gray walls. All these were proud creations of Shawn's grandmother, Ruth, whose spotless home could be easily confused with a museum if the furniture went missing.

A golden birdcage hung in the corner of the room near the window. Inside, the yellow and green lovebirds, Sunny and Cloudy, nestled against each other. Shawn dropped a large spoonful of cooked lentils into their feeding trough. His grandmother liked to stick her fingers into the cage to caress their feathers., But Shawn only dared to feed them. Nothing more.

Shawn kicked his feet up onto the walnut coffee table and tried to sink into the red velvet couch, but it never let him. It was too much like his grandmother, stiff and proper. He turned on the TV and flipped through the channels until he settled on a black and white movie, where a woman gritted her teeth while a seamstress worked on zipping up the back of her wedding dress. The woman turned toward a mirror, and her face lit up. The seamstress dabbed a tear from her cheek.

Ruth's voice echoed from her bedroom down to the hall. "Shawn, I can hear your feet on the table."

Shawn quickly moved his legs off the table. "You can't hear feet."

Ruth glided into the room in a vintage robe. She was in her seventies with curly auburn hair and a slim body, a gift from her years of swimming. Her stateliness masked her artistic side. She never traveled without putting her face on, as she called it.

"Bore me with the details," she said.

Shawn looked away from her inquisitive eyes at the darkening clouds outside. It felt like the sun was forever setting on his dating life.

Ruth tapped her foot. "I'm waiting."

"Same as always…"

Ruth frowned. "You didn't look into her eyes, did you?"

Shawn looked at the floor. "No one's going to marry me."

"Marry? We need to get you a second date." She straightened one of the paintings on the wall.

"If I don't get married, I won't have anyone after you die."

"I'm still ticking. And when I'm not, you'll have your brother, whatever that's worth."

"Sometimes, to keep myself going, I picture you lying in a casket."

Ruth gasped. "How dare you say that. You know I want to be cremated. So, no one can screw up my makeup."

"Maybe I should start picturing you as an urn."

Ruth shrugged. "Whatever works."

Shawn glanced out the window. A breeze rustled through the trees in Central Park. A drizzle fell in sheets from the sky. "I miss Grandpa."

"Yeah? Me too." Ruth filled a silver teapot with water from the sink and set it on the stove. "He'd love to ask me about my day and then turn off his hearing aid." Ruth snickered. "Once, he told me the best part of growing up was getting less and less peer pressure since all his peers were dying."

"He died so suddenly. I don't want that to happen to you."

"That's sweet, Shawn," she said, walking toward him. She took an unsteady step and grabbed a nearby chair to get her balance.

"Who'll buy my cereal? Or help me pay bills? Or…"

"Glad I'll be missed," she said with a wry smile. "Just promise me you'll keep the urn polished."

"Of course."

Shawn returned his attention to the TV. The woman was dolled up for her wedding day, gliding down a sweeping staircase. The groom's smile stretched from one ear to the other. Shawn imagined himself in that white suit, waiting for the love of his life.

"Tell me about your wedding day again, Grandma."

Ruth didn't answer.

Shawn looked over and saw her slumped in her rocking chair, looking like a marionette without its strings. "Grandma?" His mouth went dry. He rushed over and shook her, but she only flopped around in his hands.

# CHAPTER 2

## PICKY ABOUT THE GUESTS

Shawn gripped the metal bar on the inside of the ambulance as it wove through the traffic-jammed Manhattan streets toward Mt. Sinai Hospital. His insides quivered. The brawny paramedic inserted an IV into his grandmother's arm as she lay still on the stretcher. Shawn shut his ears to the piercing WHUP, WHUP of the ambulance siren.

Hours later, Shawn wrung his hands as he sat in a chair next to his grandma and prayed silently. She was asleep in her hospital bed in a room she shared with a frail woman who needed a machine to breathe. A pale-yellow curtain separated them. Ruth looked fragile in her seafoam-colored hospital gown, under the loud fluorescent lights. The air felt still and was quiet, except for the beeps and wooshes from the various machines surrounding her bed.

A sturdy doctor entered the room, holding Ruth's chart. In his late forties, he had deep-set eyes and graying hair, with a kind face behind round glasses. He wore boots, probably to give himself some extra height. The doctor walked over to Shawn and glanced at Ruth with a concerned look. "When you get to her age, things can start breaking down fast," he said with a sigh.

Shawn shushed him. "Praying." The doctor nodded and checked his watch. After a moment, Shawn raised his head and motioned for the doctor to continue. Before he could, the sizable white door to the room swung open, and Colin rushed inside. He was in his thirties, with a narrow face and spiky blond hair; he was scruffy but appeared easygoing.

Colin started to hug Shawn but stopped himself.

"Panic attack?" Colin asked.

"Diabetes. Grandma's blood sugar was too low. She passed out," Shawn told him.

"She needs to monitor herself to stay healthy. Especially at her age," the doctor said.

"That's what they said to Grandpa," Shawn said. "I thought he did until he took a nap and didn't wake up."

"He also had diabetes?" the doctor asked. Shawn and Colin both nodded.

"Grandpa always told us, when life hands you lemons, diabetics should not make lemonade," Colin said. "He also liked to say the reason he married Grandma was because she was his type. Type 1 diabetes."

The doctor didn't smile. "Well, you have to stay on top of it one day at a time. Make sure she's drinking enough fluids and monitoring herself. She should be ready to go by tomorrow."

Colin motioned to the patient on the other side of the curtain. "I heard that woman swallowed a hundred-dollar bill." The doctor glanced at the woman and then back to Colin, confused. Leaning in, Colin lowered his voice. "Has there been any change?" Colin laughed, but the doctor shook his head and made his way out of the room.

"Was that a joke?" Shawn asked him.

"If you have to ask, I'm not doing it right," Colin said.

"I don't think this is the time to be funny."

Colin wrinkled his nose. "This is exactly when we need jokes. You know Grandpa would be cracking a few."

Shawn pulled the covers closer to Ruth's neck, tucking her in. "If we lose Grandma…"

Colin texted on his phone. "Like the doctor said. One day at a time,

Shawn."

"I always thought she'd see me get married before she passed away."

"Better hurry up then," Colin said with a twinkle in his eyes. Shawn glared at him. "I'm kidding. Kidding. But I'm kind of not kidding, too." Colin returned to his texting.

Shawn's shoulders slumped as if the weight of everything was finally bearing down on him. "I asked a girl to go out this weekend, but she told me she was going to have a headache. I don't know how she'd know that."

Colin scrolled through a few emails on his phone. "I'll give you some pointers."

"I need more than that."

"Doesn't your dating app job help out in that department?" Colin asked.

"Not as much as I thought it would." Shawn sighed.

After they left the hospital, Colin assured Shawn that he would spend the night at Ruth's place and take on their grandma's role while she was away, but he bought the wrong cereal and ruined the next morning. Shawn took a taxi back to the hospital and brought Ruth home shortly afterward.

They made it back into their home, where Shawn helped arrange the pillows on Ruth's bed so she would be comfortable.

"I'm perfectly fine. I don't know what all the fuss is about," Ruth said as she reclined against the pillows and picked up a book.

"I just want you alive as long as possible," Shawn said.

"That's God's department," Ruth said. Shawn sighed and left for work.

Shawn had landed his job at an elite dating app, Exclusiv, thinking it would skyrocket his possibilities of finding his future wife, but he felt stuck on the launching pad. It was rare for him to get past the first date, and when he did, it was unlikely he'd be granted another one.

Shawn was always the first one at his desk every day. He liked getting to the office before everyone else so he could organize his desk, push in his earplugs, and get busy writing code for their app distraction-free.

While he thought he was alone in the office, he sometimes said "hello" to the pictures of the freakishly happy couples plastered on the walls around the office. However, he stopped doing that right after he heard a "hello" back from someone who had beat him to the office that morning. Shawn was the butt of a few jokes during that day's lunch break.

Taped to the walls surrounding Shawn's desk were neatly arranged pictures of happily married couples he had cut out from different magazines or printed from his favorite wedding websites. In one photo, a groom carried his bride across the threshold of their front door. In another, a married couple locked lips at the end of a pier. Another snapshot featured a newly hitched couple waving from the backseat of a taxi. Looking at those scenes filled Shawn with hope and made him feel warm all over.

Sometimes, Shawn would close his eyes and pretend he was one of the men in those pictures. Then he'd lose track of time. One morning, Shawn even nodded off. Now he only allowed himself to imagine himself in those scenes when he felt especially lonely.

The employees in the other workstations around him were good-looking, mostly in their twenties, and they frequently met up for drinks after work and failed to invite Shawn. They were often glued to their phones, and Shawn wondered if they were masking their socializing and gaming as work. Sometimes Shawn wondered how the dating app kept going since it seemed like he was the only one doing any real work. But it did, so they must be doing something.

When Shawn first started working at Exclusiv, he tried to engage in conversations with his coworkers. He'd force himself to look into their eyes while he drummed up interesting facts about dating apps or love in general. Before long, his coworkers didn't have time to talk to him, and it became too much work for him to try to connect. He resorted to a quick "hello" in the elevator, and they were fine with that.

Jammed between two of the pictures above his desk was one of Shawn's favorite verses from the Bible written across a blue index card: "I waited patiently for the Lord; He turned to me and heard my cry." The card was a note to him from Amanda, whom he dated in college.

Their relationship lasted past the second date, and he never wanted to forget her. When he held the card close, he could still make out a trace of her perfume. Or at least he convinced himself he could.

Shawn preferred being isolated in his corner workstation. His desk was always clutter-free, which kept him focused on typing the right code into his computer to keep the app running smoothly. He was always dressed in his standard outfit of a plain polo and jeans. The shirt colors rotated depending on the day: pale blue was Monday, dark green Tuesday, light orange Wednesday, dark purple Thursday, gray Friday, black Saturday, and muted red Sunday. Then he'd repeat the cycle. He stayed away from more intense colors because their sounds could overpower him if he gazed at them too long.

That day, out of the corner of his eye, Shawn peered at Flynn, who sat at his desk a few feet away in all his headphone-wearing, hipster glory, wearing a plaid shirt and skinny jeans.

The women in the office seemed to pass by Flynn's desk the most often, and Shawn took note of that. Shawn also followed Flynn online, where his feeds were always filled with pictures of him with his arms wrapped around gorgeous women or with good-looking friends, at parties or dinners, sometimes on a yacht. Shawn sometimes wanted Flynn's life.

Flynn scrolled through photos of females from their dating app on his computer. Their boss, Jake, emerged from his glass-enclosed office a few doors down the hall. Jake's smile resembled the Cheshire cat. In his late forties, he was tall and toned but tried too hard to look young, tan, and current. He approached Flynn while Shawn pulled out his earplugs to listen. Jake motioned to the many female faces flashing by on Flynn's computer. "Flynn, my man. How fresh is the meat?"

Flynn's face wrinkled with disappointment. "A little rotten."

Jake watched the screen and grimaced as various women zipped by. "Maybe we should just be a free-for-all and let ugly people mate like everyone else. They're people, too. Aren't they?" Flynn shrugged. Shawn winced. He didn't like hearing his boss talk that way.

What made Exclusiv so exclusive was how they monitored the offerings and booted out anyone who didn't fit the app's ideals, or more accurately, Jake's ideals. It was a badge of honor if you were accepted by the app and something you didn't mention if you weren't.

A picture of a well-endowed ex-cheerleader type caught Jake's attention. "Who's this hottie?" he asked, clicking on her profile. Below her picture was a red number six inside a blue circle. He turned to Shawn. "Why is she rated a six?"

Shawn moved closer to Flynn's computer and glanced at the screen. "Because she lied in her profile."

Jake looked back at the computer, then at Shawn. "Your system is a lie detector?"

"She says she majored in cosmetology. At Harvard. Not possible. My algorithm cross-checked the way she—"

Jake interrupted. "And you wonder why we haven't launched your rating system yet? Somebody who looks like this should have a boost to their score."

Shawn raised an eyebrow. "The score is objective. It's her history of how many times she—"

"Nobody cares about histories if we lose all the young and hot with valid credit cards." Jake put his hands on his hips. "Let's find a way to reward this beauty."

Shawn wrinkled his forehead and rubbed the back of his neck. "You might have a point."

"Of course I do." Jake let out a huff and made his way back to his office. Flynn reached for his headphones and disappeared back into his world.

Shawn cleared his throat until Flynn looked up and took off his headphones. "Um, my account was erased again," Shawn said.

"Oh, yeah. New rule. Employees can't use our app anymore," Flynn said, fiddling with his leather bracelet.

"But you are."

Flynn smiled. "For quality control."

"What about Adele?"

"Uh, same thing."

"And Cyrus?"

Flynn frowned and shook his head. "Shawn, I'm sorry. We've had a few complaints from the girls you met. Actually, all the girls you met." Shawn's expression turned to concern. Flynn softened. "Not a big deal.

But maybe you can try some other apps."

"I know my chances of finding someone will go up if I can—"

"Sorry, man," Flynn said, turning back to his computer and snapping his headphones back on.

Shawn wondered if he should say anything else, then decided to let it go for now. Knowing he could get fixated on what he thought was important, he returned to his desk, feeling an ache in the pit of his stomach. He was either hungry or lonely. Or both. He longed to be more like Flynn. Everything seemed to come easy to him.

Tammy made her way through the workstations, dropping off envelopes. She was in her mid-twenties, pretty but edgy, blond with streaks of a darker color, hiding her figure under T-shirts that shouted her causes. That day's shirt read 'FUR is Dead.' She handed Flynn an envelope. "Passes for the women haters' ball."

"You mean our promo party?" Flynn asked.

Tammy clenched her jaw. "Open your eyes." She seemed to be used to that kind of reaction from her coworkers whenever she woke them up with a splash of reality. From her objections, you would think she was the only one who really cared about what was happening in the world. When others complained about the cost of a gym membership, she complained about the lack of clean water in Africa.

When Tammy first started working at Exclusiv, her coworkers invited her out to drinks, but she wanted to keep a safe distance. When people asked her about how she met Jake and where she worked previously, she turned the conversation into what they could do to make the world a better place. Soon, rumors started flying around the office about who Tammy was and why she was hired. As long as they didn't figure it out, she didn't care.

Shawn glanced up at Tammy, looking hopeful for an invite. She kept walking. "Sorry, Shawn. Jake is picky about the guests," she said.

"What if I don't eat or drink anything?" Shawn asked, looking like a dog begging for scraps.

Tammy looked him over, and pity got the better of her. She snuck an envelope to Shawn while putting on a show for the benefit of her coworkers. "Can't do it, Shawn. You know when Jake says 'no,' he means 'no'." She stared daggers at the others in the office. "Kind of like victims of sexual assault. No means no, people!"

A few people groaned around the office, as this wasn't her first mini-lecture. Shawn looked between the envelope and Tammy with a blank look. "If I can't go, who's this for?"

Tammy moved close enough to Shawn so the others couldn't hear. He could smell her musk perfume but didn't say anything. "I hate the theme and object to it on principle, but I hope to see you there. You can bring a guest but avoid Jake and make sure you're in costume." She started to say more but stopped herself.

Shawn pulled the invite out of the envelope and examined the puffy 1970s style font that announced, 'Pimps and Hos Party!' He knew the only way he could go was if he didn't reveal the theme to his grandma. She would definitely get upset, and she might lose track of her blood sugar levels again if he brought up the theme.

He'd have to tell her he was off to a work party, which was true. She'd be happy to know Shawn would be getting another chance to meet someone special.

# CHAPTER 3

## PIMPS AND HOS

Shawn crept toward the door of his grandma's apartment, hoping she wouldn't notice he was dressed in velvet pajamas.

"Leaving already?" Ruth asked. "Promise me you'll be careful. I don't like feeling anxious when you're gone."

"Of course, I'll be careful."

Ruth opened the side table drawer next to the front door and pulled out the thick family Bible. It had a blue and gold cover and a latch on one side that held the gold-edged pages shut. Ruth placed Shawn's hand on top of the Bible. "Promise me again."

"You're being ridiculous," Shawn said. He begrudgingly put his hand on the Bible since he knew that was the only way she'd let this go. "I promise to be careful."

"I feel much better now."

Whenever Shawn had noticed his grandpa reading that same Bible, his grandpa would always announce he was "looking for loopholes." But Shawn knew better. Every Sunday, Grandpa had faithfully attended church with Grandma. Now that Grandpa was gone, Shawn took his place by her side.

Shawn stood on the curb in front of a large warehouse where techno music boomed. The Manhattan Bridge stretched overhead with the city as its jeweled backdrop. Men and women dressed as 1970s pimps and hos mingled and laughed as they passed by Shawn to line up at the warehouse entrance. A burly man dressed from head to toe in black leather took passes at the door and unhitched the velvet rope to allow people inside.

Dressed in a ruby smoking jacket and velvet pajamas, Shawn shifted his weight from one leg to the other, doing his best to look comfortable but failing miserably.

"What's up, bro?" Shawn turned to see Colin dressed in a shimmery gold suit, white platform shoes, giant glasses, and a feathered hat.

"This is a pimps and hos party. Why are you dressed like Elton John?" Shawn asked.

Colin looked over his outfit, nodding. "I should've asked myself in the mirror." He shrugged and pointed to Shawn's outfit. "And you are…"

"Hugh Hefner. He was the ultimate pimp." Shawn beamed proudly. "I read that online."

"Surprised Grandma didn't give you a hard time."

"She made me swear on the Bible."

"Typical. You get away with a lot more than I did when I lived there," Colin said.

They strolled toward the warehouse. "Not really," Shawn said as he put in earplugs. "I'm just not as obvious as you were."

Shawn and Colin made it past the velvet rope and pushed their way through the crush of colorful pimps and hos who mingled around the warehouse, shouting to be heard above the music. The women wore a range of styles, from tight miniskirts to barely anything at all, complemented with fishnet or torn stockings, stilettos, or thigh-high boots. The men were dressed in colorful suits with bell-bottom pants, some donning oversized Afro wigs. One of the men kept his 'hos' on a studded leash, which Shawn found disturbing.

"I need to hit the restroom," Colin said. "I'll meet you back here."

Shawn nodded and watched Colin wedge into the crowd. He scoped the room and noticed a woman in a polka dot mini skirt and beaded wig sipping her drink nearby. This was his chance. He made his way over to her. "I sure hope we don't have to ration gas," Shawn said.

"Excuse me?" the woman asked with a confused look on her face.

"That's what America had to do when OPEC embargoed oil in 1973. Then we had to do it again after the Iranian Revolution." Shawn wiped his forehead. It suddenly felt scorching hot, and butterflies were partying in his stomach.

The woman's face tightened as her eyes focused on Shawn. "I need a refill." She strode away with a completely full drinking glass. *If she realized most people at this party are in 1970s costumes, she would've appreciated my geopolitical references.*

A tall blond woman who reminded Shawn of a grown-up version of a Barbie doll stood hunched over a few feet away, texting on her phone. *Here's my chance.* Shawn got close enough so she'd notice him.

"You have to hold your phone directly in front of your face when you're texting," Shawn said.

"You're talking to me?" Barbie asked.

Nodding, Shawn motioned to her phone. "Text neck. It's a thing that happens when people lean over to use their phones. It causes too much strain."

The woman raised her eyebrows. "Never heard of text neck."

"It's a thing."

"Are you a doctor?"

"No, but I've been to many of them."

Barbie pointed across the room. "I gotta meet up with someone."

Shawn came very close to asking her if his name was Ken, but he resisted. "I can go with you."

"We need to talk in private. Sorry. It's a thing."

Shawn stepped back and pulled at his collar. "Of course. Go ahead. No big deal."

She turned away, gliding through the crowd. She stopped next to one of the bars and continued texting. Shawn waited but didn't see anyone join her. Undaunted, he approached a woman with long red curly hair huddled in a group with two other ladies.

"Can I interest you in some conversation?" he asked. "I can explore a variety of topics."

"No hablo Ingles." She turned back to the two women in her group and talked to them in perfect English. *So strange.*

Colin returned with a grin on his face. "This party is very similar to a dream I had the other night. Except all the guests were chasing me until I fell down a hole. Then I was falling and falling until I woke up."

"That's an odd dream."

"Let's avoid any holes." Colin motioned for Shawn to follow him.

"Look who showed up." Tammy approached them, dressed in a slim black dress featuring a bright graphic of a traffic light.

"You look like a stoplight," Shawn said, pointing to her dress.

Tammy nodded, smiling. "Exactly. Stop human trafficking."

Shawn looked over her dress, confused. "What does that have to do with the party?"

Tammy put her hands on her hips. "You think 'hos' are 'hos' by choice? It's not a choice if you couldn't stop the sexual abuse when you were a kid. We shouldn't be celebrating women being trafficked by pimps."

"You're kind of intense," Colin said.

"Modern slavery is intense," Tammy said. She gestured to the people around the room. "But these people only care about being drunk, sexy, and fun."

Colin eyed the room. "Not a bad way to spend the night."

"All I see is sweaty, insecure, and desperate," Tammy said with a sigh. "A lot of Me Too moments happening here." She looked at Shawn. "But I know you're different. Enjoy the party." She pushed her way through the crowd.

"She likes to ask questions but doesn't give you time to answer," Shawn said.

They continued onward, toward a bar at the center of the room where several bartenders dressed in black strained to hear the shouted requests from the throng of people surrounding them. Shawn and

Colin squeezed in behind the crowd of people to wait their turn.

Shawn looked around, biting his lip. He wished he could push a fast-forward button to speed through the night. The room felt like it was going to swallow him. The music became excessively loud. The swirling, colored lights beaming down from the ceiling seemed to grow brighter. The voices and music fused together and became deafening. Shawn wrung his hands and gazed off into the distance. He felt a sour taste in his mouth.

Colin noticed Shawn zoning out. "You okay, bro?" Shawn forced a smile. "Just breathe. Concentrate on one thing at a time. Free food, free drinks, lots of eye candy. Feels like Christmas to me." Three ladies in tight, revealing outfits sashayed by them. "Ho, ho, and ho."

Shawn noticed them too, his eyebrows drawing together. "The way these women are dressed will increase the chances of unwanted pregnancy."

Colin laughed like he always did when Shawn pointed out what others noticed but would never say.

Jake approached the bar in a red velvet suit and gold chains. Shawn turned away from him but not quickly enough.

"Shawn?" Jake asked.

Shawn jumped, then hurried away. Jake quickly caught up to him while Colin watched with a curious look on his face.

"I'm not eating or drinking," Shawn said.

"It's okay. Relax. I never thought you'd want to attend our par-tays. You get mad when we breathe too loud," Jake said.

Shawn took a deep breath. "Can't find my soulmate if I just sit at home."

"Actually, you can. That's the point of our app." Jake glanced around the room. "Well, you're surrounded by oysters. Time to find your pearl."

"My pearl?"

Jake groaned, then pulled out his wallet. He waved a one-hundred-dollar bill in front of Shawn's face. "Let's make this interesting. This is yours if you get a date with any of these hos."

A slow smile spread across Colin's face as he approached them. "Easy money."

Jake grinned. "Oh yeah? Wanna make it a bet?"

Shawn shook his head, but Colin winked at him as if he had a better plan. "Sure."

"Better get moving then. Or you're making me a hundred bucks richer." Jake wore a satisfied look on his face as he sauntered away.

Shawn looked over to Colin, shuffling his feet. "That's a lot of money."

"You're up for the challenge."

That moment brought back memories of Atlantic City. Colin thought it would be an adventure to trek out to the casinos on his twenty-first birthday to try his luck at blackjack. Not exactly luck. He was hoping Shawn could count the cards and tell him when to say, "Hit me." He got the idea from watching *Rain Man*. But it turned out Shawn didn't have those same skills. Colin spent the rest of the weekend searching for quiet places where Shawn wouldn't feel deluged by all the lights and activity. That was their last trip to a casino.

Colin peered around the room for a possible candidate for Shawn. "What about her?" Colin nodded to a tall, curvy woman with chestnut hair who leaned against the wall, sipping her drink. She glanced their way. Colin caught her eye and nodded. "She's kinda flirty. Turn on your charm." Shawn stood with his arms at his sides, unsure what to do. Colin nudged him. "Smile back."

Shawn smiled big. Way too big. "No. Stop. Get her attention, don't make her think you're running for office. Try something more subtle. Like this." Colin formed his lips into a faint smile.

Shawn mirrored Colin's smile and pivoted toward the woman. Except he kept smiling as if he was hatching an evil plan. Colin waved at him to stop. "Creepy. Creepy. Don't smile the whole time. Just long enough to hook her, not make her blow the rape whistle."

Shawn clammed up, not sure how long that was supposed to be.

Colin nodded. "Three seconds tops. Turn your head, smile for three seconds, then turn back. Try it."

Shawn took a breath and set his watch. He turned his head, smiled, started the timer—one, two, three. Then he turned his head back and dropped the smile.

Colin beamed. "That was amazing."

They glanced over to the woman. Her mouth was agape. She was either impressed by the magnitude of Shawn's smile or completely horrified; it was hard to tell. She quickly dove into the crowd. Colin's shoulders slumped in defeat. "Well, what's a hundred dollars?"

"It's a lot of money," Shawn said, wringing his hands.

"I'll pay half."

"But it was your idea."

"Fine, but I'm going to find another place for us to go. This place is dead." Colin scrolled through his phone while Shawn scanned the crowd; he wasn't ready to give up. He saw a few faces and tried the three-second smile with no results.

Then he saw her.

She was in her early twenties with dirty blond hair that tickled her shoulders. Her angular face was beautiful, with eyes the color of jade. She was dressed in a white velvet tube top, tiny white skirt, and thigh-high white boots. Heavy makeup covered her face, which made her look older, harder, but there was a glimmer of sweetness there.

Shawn waved to her and did his three-second smile. She stopped and peered at him as if she had just realized he was smiling at her. Then she started walking toward him. "It worked!" he whisper-shouted to Colin, who glanced over and saw her approaching.

"Nice work," Colin said. He gave Shawn a friendly push toward her and stepped away.

The woman reached Shawn, chewing her gum, and gave him a nod and a wink while Colin watched from a safe distance. Shawn pointed to her white tube top. "White is the color of all wavelengths of visible light. People think black is all colors, but black is the absence of color."

She tilted her head, curious. Then she blew a big green bubble until it popped. Wiping the gum back into her mouth, she eyed Shawn up and down. "I'm Violet."

Shawn stood a little taller. "A color on the higher end of the visible spectrum. I'm Shawn. Would you like to go on a date with me?"

Violet laughed. "You always that quick?" She combed her fingers through her hair and looked him over, leaning a hand on her right hip. "We can go someplace right now." She popped another bubble.

"I can't right now."

"We can do later, but it'll cost you." Violet gave him a sly wink. "You're at a pimps and hos party. Talking to an actual 'ho.'"

He shook his head, confused. "I'm not good at pretend."

Violet stroked her neck. "And I'm good at everything as long as I'm paid by the hour."

Shawn leaned closer to her. "I used to be paid by the hour. Now I'm on salary."

"Three hundred an hour. But I promise I'm worth it." She blew another green bubble.

Shawn's eyes opened wide with curiosity. "What do you do to earn that much?"

"Like I said. Everything," Violet licked her upper lip. Shawn wondered if she was thirsty.

He thought through his week. "You free Saturday night?"

She moved a little closer to him. "That's my most popular night." He could smell her minty breath as she traced the opening of her tube top with her fingers. "What time do you wanna start?"

"I don't know. Seven o'clock?"

"For how long?"

This was the first time Shawn had been asked all these specifics about a potential date. He hoped he wouldn't say anything to mess it up.

"Until ten?"

Violet looked him over and batted her eyelashes. "I'm not cheap."

"I didn't think you were," Shawn said, unsure why she so quickly thought he'd jump to that conclusion.

Violet moistened her lips. "So, you're a big spender."

Shawn crossed his arms. "Not really. If we lasted that long, it would be a new record for me."

"Not for me. Text me your address." She handed him a business card. It was white and only said Violet with a phone number and an email.

Shawn took it and smiled back at her, pushing his chest out. "I look forward to going out."

She let out a quick sigh. "Going somewhere is extra."

"Oh. Then we can stay in. My grandma can make us something."

Shawn liked that she was thinking about his budget.

Violet tilted her head to the side. "Your grandma will be part of this?"

Shawn clasped his hands together. "She'll be so excited. I hope that's okay."

"We'll see." She gave him another wink and a seductive lip lick. "I'll bring dessert."

"I like chocolate," he said, his face filling with excitement. "But dark. I can't have milk chocolate."

Violet stopped chewing her gum and nodded blankly. She wasn't used to getting this kind of reaction from the men she encountered. Most guys would've left the party with her right away. This one had patience she hadn't seen before.

"Looking forward to it," Violet said. Then she turned and got lost in the crowd. Shawn watched her go while the music roared back into his mind, and the lights around him sparkled brightly, like miniature suns floating throughout the room.

Colin approached him with a pleased look on his face. "Hey, bro. We won a hundred bucks." Shawn couldn't care less about the money. His eyes sparkled and gleamed. He had something much better: a date.

# CHAPTER 4

## THE GIRLFRIEND EXPERIENCE

Shawn's grandma worked in overdrive to do everything she could to make sure Shawn's date would be a success. She wore an apron over her silk nightgown as she hustled around her kitchen, putting spices into a pot of chili boiling on the stove. This was the first time she had a front-row seat for one of Shawn's dates. She took a long afternoon nap, so she'd be on top of her game.

"Plates. Forks, knives, spoons, napkins," she mumbled to herself. "What else? What else?"

"You're sure chili is the way to go, Grandma?" Shawn asked, wrinkling his nose.

"It's hearty. Healthy. Easy to eat. It's what your grandpa and I had on our first date. Of course, that was in the middle of a blizzard." She stirred the chili and looked lost in the moment. "We were stuck in SoHo and stepped into the Landmark diner to thaw. Chili was just the thing. Your grandpa took a bite. He saw a basil leaf in his bowl and told me he hoped we'd get to third basil."

Shawn shrugged. "I don't know what that means."

Ruth laughed. "Just make sure you keep looking into her eyes.

Women like that."

"I'll do my best," Shawn said, looking away from her. Ruth handed him drinking glasses, and he carefully placed them on the table. Then they heard a knock on the door. Shawn's eyes got wide, and he wrung his hands. "She's actually here."

"Of course she is."

"Sometimes they don't show up and don't give a reason."

"You'll be okay," Ruth said in a reassuring voice.

Shawn looked down at his green polo shirt. "I should've worn the orange shirt. That's the one for special occasions." He felt an empty feeling in the pit of his stomach.

"You look fine." Ruth put her chin up and stepped over to the door. She gave Shawn a thumbs up and opened the door slowly to find Violet on the other side in a tank top, tight purple skirt, fishnet stockings, and a pair of impossible heels. She gave Ruth an empty smile, clutching her knock-off Louis Vuitton bag and a long coat.

"You must be the grandma. I thought he was joking," Violet said, biting her lower lip.

"It's hard for me to joke," Shawn yelled from the kitchen. "I'm glad you made it."

Ruth's eyes narrowed on Violet's wardrobe. "Women certainly dress edgy these days."

"I do my best." Violet let herself into the living room and draped her coat across the edge of the couch. "I've never done anything like this before."

"Anything like what?" Ruth asked as she shut the door.

"I have rules," Violet said, rubbing her hands together. "No touching until I say it's okay. And if I don't want to do something, I won't. And no pictures."

"I've always thought bashfulness is an attractive quality," Ruth said to Violet with a wink. "Most women today have terrible boundaries. I like you already." She turned to Shawn. "Everything should be ready. You know what to do. You two enjoy yourselves. I'll be in bed."

"Oh, we will," Violet said as she twisted one of the rings on her finger.

"I'll see you soon." Ruth kissed Shawn on his cheek and retreated to her bedroom at the end of the hall. Violet's eyes darted around the room.

"You forgot dessert," Shawn said with a puzzled look.

Violet motioned to herself. "It's right here."

Shawn looked at Violet and her coat but still couldn't see anything. Shrugging, he ushered her over to the table. A cautious smile crept across Violet's face as she looked over everything.

"Dinner? You were serious," Violet said, stepping closer to the table.

Shawn shuffled his feet. "People tell me I can be too serious."

Violet nodded and grasped the back of one of the dining room chairs. "Oh, you want the girlfriend experience?"

Shawn gave Violet a quick glance then looked away. "As long as it leads to something more."

Violet ran her fingers up her arm. "Oh, it will. We can role-play whatever you want."

Shawn pulled out one of the chairs from the table. "Are you hungry?"

Violet's voice dropped a register into a sultry zone. "I'm very hungry." She picked up a muffin and held it in the palm of her hand. "Ooooh, muffins." She took a long seductive lick of the muffin, winking at him.

"You wink a lot," Shawn said.

"Mmmmm. Apple." Violet started to return the muffin but then decided to eat it instead. She brushed the crumbs off her tank top as she devoured it in a few bites. Violet usually had a whole routine with new clients, and baked goods were not a part of it. Something was off about their interaction, but she didn't know what. She finished off the muffin.

"The apple is the official fruit for New York state. Dried apples were a staple for the early colonists."

"You like to talk a lot. Whatever makes you happy." She made her way down the hallway while Shawn watched with a baffled look on his face.

"I'll let you know when I'm ready," Violet said as she stepped into Shawn's room.

A bride and groom bobblehead peered out from the shelf above Shawn's desk in his highly organized room. They had flat faces with plastic sleeves so couples could insert their own pictures for the heads. The groom held a picture of Shawn's face, but the bride's face stood blank. Shawn was waiting to fill it in with an image of his eventual wife. The bobbleheads were a Christmas gift from Colin from years ago, though Shawn had since taped the back of their heads to keep them from continually nodding.

Computer programming books lined the wall above his twin-sized bed. Board games and comic books were stacked neatly next to his desk, including Shawn's favorite game book, *You're Pulling My Leg!*, which featured over six hundred get-to-know-you questions. Shawn also kept a version he could read on his phone to easily bring it with him on dates and give himself ideas on how to keep the conversation moving.

Violet shook her head with dread when she noticed a picture of Ruth with her arm around Shawn in a frame at the end of the shelf. She picked up an ant farm kit from Shawn's desk and looked at the tunnels the ants had burrowed into the sand. "You like ants?" she shouted.

"They're very productive. Ants can carry fifty times their weight," Shawn yelled from the living room.

Violet pulled back the Star Wars sheets on the bed, then grabbed a small bottle of perfume from her bag, spraying a few puffs into the air. She whipped off her tank top, revealing a snake tattoo down her back. "We should get the business part out of the way first."

She turned away from the door to slide the perfume back in her purse as Shawn walked in. "The business part?"

At the sight of her naked back, his jaw dropped. He darted his eyes and backed into the desk, knocking the groom bobblehead off the shelf and dislodging the tape. He caught it and used it to shield his eyes. "I'm so sorry. I didn't know you were changing."

The way he held the bobblehead made it look like it was doing the talking. An amused smile broke across Violet's face as Shawn tried to make his way out of the room. He bumped into the doorframe, slammed the bobblehead onto the desk, and rushed out. Violet slipped her top back on. For once, she was going too quickly.

Shawn rushed to the kitchen sink and splashed water onto his face. He squeezed his eyes closed and took a deep breath. Then he toweled off his face.

Violet returned to the living room, looking at him through her long eyelashes. "You're new at this. I get it. Not a big deal." She leaned against the couch. "You booked me for three hours, handsome. We've got some time. But before we begin, I need nine hundred."

Shawn turned to her with a blank look on his face. "Nine hundred what?"

Violet looked him over and eyed the front door. "Are you a cop?"

Shawn straightened up. "I'm a computer programmer. For a dating app. I turn original formulations into executable programs, solve problems resulting in an algorithm, verify requirements of the algorithm including its correctness and its resource consumption, implementation of the algorithm—"

"I'd love to hear more about that later," Violet said, tapping her fingers on her leg.

Shawn looked down at the floor. "I'd really have to show you."

"You're the one who hired me. You can show me whatever you want." Violet paced back and forth, keeping her eyes fixed on Shawn. When her clients stalled, bad things usually happened. She had to get her john to pay, or she would be the one who would pay later.

Shawn raised his eyebrows and looked at her intently. "I don't understand. Why would I hire you?" Stepping over to the table, Shawn spooned chili into a bowl and placed it across from him. Then he filled another bowl.

Violet watched, tilting her head to the side. "So, this was an actual date."

Shawn smiled. "Of course it's a date. What else would it be?" He sprinkled a handful of cheese onto his chili.

Violet took in the setting—the table, the candles, the food. She looked at him as though suddenly realizing something was different about him. "What do you think I am?"

Shawn shifted uncomfortably as he looked her over. "You're a pretty woman."

Violet peered into his eyes for a moment, affected by him. He couldn't hold her look for long. She had been in situations before when the john pretended he didn't know what was going on, sometimes to get out of paying her and other times because of guilt. But this guy was different. He seemed genuinely perplexed.

Shawn picked up one of the muffins and took a bite. "I can tell you really like muffins. The apple muffin is also the official muffin for New York State."

Violet snapped back to reality. She pulled out her phone and typed something into it. Shawn watched her, rocking on his feet. "You don't believe me?"

"It's not that. I need to let my guy know what's going on."

"Your guy?"

Violet finished texting. She heard a chirp and noticed the covered cage in the corner of the room. "You've got some pets."

"Sunny and Cloudy."

"Excuse me?"

"Two lovebirds."

Violet stepped closer to the cage. "Real lovebirds?"

Shawn nodded. "When Cloudy threw up, we figured out he was the male. The males always feed the nesting female. With vomit."

Violet winced. "Even birds don't know how to treat their women."

"No, she likes it."

"Trust me. She doesn't." Her phone buzzed, and she read the screen. "Gotta go."

Shawn blushed. "What about our date?"

Violet felt sorry for this clueless man, which wasn't something she typically experienced in the course of a night unless he was someone who was too ashamed to look her in her eyes but still wanted her to go through the motions. She shoved a spoonful of chili into her mouth and licked her lips. "Mmmmm. Yummy. Thank you for this wonderful date." Her face changed as she sensed something. "Did that have onions?"

Shawn nodded. She groaned, pulled out a small bottle of mouthwash from her bag, and took a swig. Walking over to the sink, she spat it out before putting on her long coat.

Shawn wrung his hands and paced back and forth. "I thought this would last a lot longer."

"That's what they all say. Sorry. I need to hook up with someone," Violet said.

"I could go with you," Shawn said with a quaking voice.

Violet raised her eyebrows. "Go with me?"

Shawn gave her a pained stare. "It's too early for our date to end. Right?"

Violet buttoned up her coat and started to get the sense that Shawn was like an eager bloodhound, and she needed to throw him off her scent. "Listen, Shawn. You should go on a date with someone else. Anyone else."

Shawn looked down. "Did I say something to hurt you? Sometimes I do that and don't realize it."

"What? No, no. It's nothing against you but—"

"You can't date a guy like me. Not the first time I've heard that." Shawn's shoulders slumped. He sat back down, defeated.

Violet's face softened, and she felt a tug on her heart. She wondered what the harm would be in letting him walk with her to her next appointment. It's always nice not to be alone. She checked the location on her phone. "This isn't too far from here."

Shawn brightened. Violet hoped she wasn't making a big mistake.

# CHAPTER 5

## AUDITIONS

Shawn led Violet out of Ruth's apartment and shut the door behind them. He carried himself with an excitement Violet hadn't seen before. Pressing the button for the elevator, Shawn grinned at her with newfound confidence. While they waited, his eyes would meet Violet's only for a moment before he darted them away.

The elevator arrived, and Violet noticed it had a bench. She wondered how that slipped her attention on the way up. She had visited high rises before but nothing this fancy. Tiny mirrors were set in between interweaving vines carved into the dark wood panels along the elevator walls. The elevator dinged, and the doors slid open.

Shawn led the way through the lobby of the building. Violet peered at the diamond-shaped lamps and the paintings of fountains adorning the walls. With a nametag labeled "Douglas," the doorman looked like he was pretending to be busy behind his desk. Douglas followed them with his eyes. He was in his sixties, handsome, with thick hair and a crooked but endearing smile.

Douglas held up a small box. "A package for your grandma."

"I'll get it on my way back," Shawn said.

"Is she doing okay?" Douglas asked.

Shawn nodded, his leg shaking. Douglas looked between Violet and Shawn. "She knows you're going out?"

Shawn beamed. "Of course she does. I'm on a date."

Douglas kept his eyes fixed on Violet as he held the door open for them. They left the apartment, turned left, and strolled up Central Park West. It was one of those rare nights when you could see a few stars peeking through the bright yellowish glow of the sky. A few joggers and neighbors walked their dogs.

Shawn looked over at Violet and took a deep, satisfied breath. "Who are you meeting?"

"Someone for work," Violet said, looking straight ahead.

Shawn hurried to keep up with her. "What do you do?"

"I'm an actress," Violet said, which was true in her mind. Most of what she did was pretending to feel something she didn't.

Shawn brightened. "Would I have seen you in something?"

"Almost." She thought of how the night could've turned out for a moment. "But, no. A lot of…auditioning." She knew she was stretching the truth and suddenly wanted her time with Shawn to end. There was no way she could shatter this poor fellow's impression of her before they parted ways.

"So, this is an audition. They happen at night?"

Violet sighed. "They happen all the time. But mostly at night." Shawn continued walking with Violet, and from the look on his face, he was still trying to figure it all out.

There was something slower about Shawn, and it was refreshing to Violet. He was a nice break from her usual conversations with men that were either direct and demeaning or filled with innuendos hinting at what the john really wanted. They sometimes talked that way to keep themselves from feeling bad about it. Violet hated when a john made her try to read his mind. She preferred when they told her what they wanted so she could get it over as quickly as possible.

They walked across 86th Street, and Violet searched the addresses until she found the right brownstone. She had been here before. Her stomach churned. "Well, I have your number." She leaned in to hug Shawn, but he pulled away.

"Sorry. Hugs. I don't…too much." Shawn kicked the ground.

"Oh. Okay. I'll see you around then." Violet waved goodbye as she walked up the steps. She buzzed the intercom while Shawn watched.

A gruff male voice crackled through the speaker. "Yeah?"

"It's me," Violet said in a friendly tone she'd use when visiting a good friend. She knew it didn't make sense, but she wanted to leave Shawn with a good impression of her. She looked back at him at the bottom of the steps and faked a smile. He waved; he wasn't afraid to hide his enthusiasm.

The door buzzed. Violet pushed it open and lingered in the doorway for a moment, glancing back at Shawn's gentle face. It wasn't the kind of face she was used to seeing. She wondered what it would be like to continue the night with Shawn instead of the guy who was going to shove a sweaty handful of twenty-dollar bills into her hands to get what was entitled to him after a long day on Wall Street.

"This is much better than a date," this john once told her while he pulled off his dark power suit. "I put out the same kind of cash. But at least with you, we have a little happy time, and I don't have to put up with all that girl chit-chat when it's over. It's like renting instead of long-term leasing, and I'm not in the market to buy."

Violet sighed, turned, and entered the bowels of the building while Shawn kept an eye on her. Opening her purse, she slipped one of her "happy" pills into her mouth to settle her stomach. Then she trudged up the stairs.

An unshaven homeless man in a stained overcoat and frayed boots picked through the recycle bin in front of the brownstone, looking for bottles. Finding one, he dropped it into the bag on his shoulder and continued on his way.

Violet stepped out of the door of the brownstone, looking worn. She checked her phone. It was late. She took a swig of her mouthwash, leaned over the stairs, and spit it out, hoping the memories of that john would go with it. Then she regained her composure and carefully walked down the steps.

"Did you get the part?"

Violet jerked her head back at seeing Shawn standing at the curb, holding two cups of coffee. "You waited?"

"I wanted to hear how it went," Shawn said with a gleam in his eye.

Violet felt a warmth in her stomach but pushed the feeling aside. *He only stayed because he thought I was someone else.* "Same as always. I just try to get through it."

Shawn handed her a cup of coffee and beamed. "Gegarang coffee. From Indonesia. I know where we can get some more."

"I like surprises, but—" She looked away from him, realizing this moment wouldn't last long. "I've got another...audition."

Shawn shuffled back a step. "You're very popular."

"I can't believe you stuck around."

"Didn't want our night to end. I hardly know you."

Violet gazed into his blue eyes and couldn't read anything beyond sincerity, even though she tried. He looked away from her, but she didn't think it was from shame. She noticed he dressed like people who came from out of town and found her through the online ads her pimp posted about her: *Looking for fun?! Hot N Sexy! Party girl looking to get together. Sweet, classy, and a little bit nasty. Fun n amazing. Gr8 at massages. Open to whatever. Generous men only.*

They started wandering down the street together. "Most people just care about my measurements," Violet said.

Shawn nodded. "We can start there." He looked her over. "How tall are you?"

She grinned. Shawn's innocence energized her. "Five-eight."

"What's your favorite cereal?"

Violet's mind flashed through several rainbow-colored cereals featuring happy bears, leprechauns, and birds. "Any sugar cereal my mom wouldn't let me have when I was growing up."

Shawn stretched his neck. "For a while, my favorite cereal was Good Friends."

"That's a cereal?"

"It used to be the only thing I ate for breakfast. Before they stopped making it. Now, I eat oatmeal."

She laughed. "That's good because you shouldn't eat Good Friends for breakfast. That's just wrong."

Shawn's grandpa once said something similar, so he knew it was a joke. He laughed.

"I'm going to invent a cereal called Enemies so people can eat their enemies for breakfast," Violet said, sipping the coffee.

"You are?"

Violet giggled, imagining the face of her pimp plastered across one of the cereal boxes. "Just a bad joke."

Shawn ran his fingers through his hair. "It helps when people explain what they mean."

Violet peered down the street and waved down a taxi. She started to feel like a kitten with her own ball of yarn. They hopped inside the cab. "Starfield Hotel on Broadway," Violet said to the driver as they headed downtown. She touched up her makeup while they navigated through the traffic. "Tourists," she said as if Shawn would understand those were her next clients.

"What about tourists?" he asked her.

Violet caught herself. "The city's jammed with them." She was used to pretending to be someone else with the men she met up with but not with someone who just wanted to spend time with her. It was a funny feeling.

When they arrived at the hotel, Violet explained she would be an hour at most since she knew that's all the time this man could afford or wanted to afford. She knew she was about to hear him drone on about how he just wanted a relaxing time away and how challenging it was to be single. Violet would do her duty and pretend there weren't wedding rings hiding somewhere in the room.

Shawn waited on a plush couch in the lobby of this hip hotel and felt a lightness in his chest. The date had gone on so long it could technically be considered their second date since she left and will be returning. That would mean he finally broke through. He decided that's how he was going to look at their time together. This was definitely a victory.

The lobby walls were lined with rows and rows of tiny blue vases, each holding a single red rose. Old typewriters dangled from the ceiling. Shawn gazed around the room at the different colors. He focused on the burnt orange velvet chair next to him until it started to hum. Moving his gaze to the brown in the painting of a bear, Shawn could hear a swishing sound. He turned to the lemon-colored lamp next to him, which beeped like a horn.

The elevator doors dinged and opened. Violet stepped out and walked through the lobby, breathing a sigh of relief. As soon as this john started crying and talking about how he wasn't the kind of man to do this sort of thing, she knew it would end quickly. When she saw Shawn, she perked up. Part of her didn't think he would wait around, but she was glad he did. She approached him, noticing he was lost in thought.

His face lit up at seeing her. "How'd you do?" he asked.

She could still feel the buzz of her pills that made it bearable. "I don't think he could tell I was acting. You okay?"

"Just listening. To the colors."

Violet looked at him with a puzzled look. Shawn looked away and clutched his hands together.

"Some of the senses in my brain are mixed up," Shawn said. "It's called synesthesia. When I look closely at colors, they can have sounds." He left out the detail of it being linked to his autism.

She peered closer at him with interest and pointed to a red rose. "What's that sound like?"

Shawn stared at the color. "Clang!"

She wrinkled her nose. "Not what I thought."

Violet sensed someone was watching her. She turned and saw Anton, who leaned against the black and white marble wall next to the glass hotel entrance. A chill raced up Violet's neck.

Anton was shadowy, in his thirties, sporting a red athletic suit. He had the barrel ribcage of a linebacker because he had been one in high school.

"I'll be right back," Violet whispered to Shawn, and that churning feeling in her stomach returned.

She approached Anton, dreading whatever he was about to say. He smacked his lips. "Productive night, sweetie?"

She dragged her nails down her cheeks. "It's been good."

"You didn't text me back."

Her heartbeat raced. She knew better than that. "I'm going there now."

Anton glanced over to Shawn with a curious look. "Who's the guy?"

"Just someone being nice to me." Violet stepped closer to Anton to keep him focused on her. She knew how he could get when something threatened her productivity.

He squeezed her shoulder. "That's my job." He gave her a quick peck on her cheek and patted her rear. "Better get a move on." He pressed himself against her and squeezed her arm tightly to remind her who's in charge. She didn't let the pain register on her face because she knew that would be a win for him. Anton thought his girls needed those reminders when they weren't quick to answer his texts, or their cash didn't add up right at the end of the night. It was just business.

She nodded. "Right."

Satisfied, Anton strutted out the front door. As he walked down the street, he noticed a frail woman whose face was withered to a collection of lines and angles. She stood hunched over on the sidewalk in a stained overcoat, displaying several worn books she was hoping to sell.

Anton dropped a fifty-dollar bill into her Styrofoam cup. The woman looked at him with awe. "God bless you."

"Make your own blessings," he said.


Violet took a moment to let her frayed nerves settle, and then she rejoined Shawn.

"Who was that?" he asked.

Violet picked a piece of lint off her shirt. "My manager." She smiled weakly as she reached into her purse. She opened her case of pills and popped one into her mouth. She caught his look. "Takes the edge off."

"You should try chamomile tea. It also relieves cramps."

Violet laughed, shocked by the remark. "Okaaay."

Shawn stood taller. "It's the glycine and hippurate."

"Um, I'll keep that in mind." She glanced at her phone with dread. "I've got one more audition."

"Great," Shawn told her, perking up.

They left the hotel together, and Violet hoped Anton was not around to notice. If he were, she knew the night wouldn't end well.

# CHAPTER 6

## WEIRD PLACE TO MEET

Violet and Shawn trekked up 6th Avenue toward 57th Street, weaving through the crowds. They passed Carnegie Hall, where well-dressed people emerged into the night air, clinging to programs and hailing cabs. They made their way up 8th Avenue, around Columbus Circle, and across 59th Street to the entrance of Central Park, dodging a few honking taxis.

They stopped beneath the grand golden statue of a general on a horse with a winged angel leading the way. The air was cold and thin, and a breeze blew through the trees that glowed orange from the streetlights.

Shawn glanced around. "This is a weird place to meet." He didn't know a lot about acting, but he now realized it wasn't as glamorous as he thought. He knew actors had to go on many auditions to land a role, but he never imagined how much effort it took or the strange places they had to go. Late in the night as well. He was glad that wasn't his life. He couldn't handle it.

Violet rubbed her hands together. "I've gotta do what I'm told."

A husky police officer plodded by them. Violet motioned for Shawn to come closer as she watched the officer continuing around the corner. "Never had good luck with cops."

"Why not?" Shawn asked.

"That's how life is for me sometimes," Violet said.

"Sorry about that."

Violet pointed to the towering globe of the world at the north end of Columbus Circle across the street. "Can you wait for me over there?"

Shawn nodded. "Sure. I hope it goes well."

"Thanks," Violet said. "It should be quick."

Shawn walked across Central Park West to the globe that towered above the entrance to the subway below. When he was a kid, Shawn used to challenge Colin to a game of seeing who could find the most countries on that globe the fastest. Shawn usually won.

He leaned against the fence next to the orb and glanced over to Violet. A short impish looking man in a loose-fitting silvery suit approached her with a twitching right hand. He must be either the director or the producer; Shawn wasn't sure. They chatted for a moment. Then, the man took her arm, and they walked down one of the darkened paths. Shawn strained to see how it was going but couldn't get a good view. Shawn glanced at his watch. He usually was in bed long before this hour.

He watched the traffic loop around the circle and whiz by him. People flowed in and out of the subway entrance below. The streets were crowded with people walking back from shows, going to catch a late movie, or getting some late-night exercise.

It always surprised Shawn that no matter what time it was, there were always people on the streets of New York City. Always. A white plastic bag fluttered to his feet before the wind whipped it across the street.

He studied the park entrance, tapping his foot. Suddenly, Violet sprinted out of the park. She darted through the oncoming cars and crossed the street. Shawn stood up, concerned.

Violet grabbed his arm and pulled him along. "There are some things I won't do for a role," she mumbled. They raced down the stairs toward the subway below. "No sense in hanging out here."

"I know where we can go," Shawn said.

They hopped on the 1 Train, rode it to 14th Street, and navigated through the tunnels. Shawn had forgotten his earplugs, so the sounds felt overwhelming. He pressed his hands against his ears as they hurried along.

"I don't like the noise either," Violet said.

They headed up the stairs and out the exit, where Shawn took a moment to catch his breath. He peeled his hands away from his ears as they continued down 8th Avenue until they arrived at Think Coffee. Inside, the pressed tin ceiling glowed with the reflected light from Ball preserving jars that had been repurposed into lamps lining the walls.

A long glass case full of cupcakes, cookies, blackberry scones, and sandwich wraps led to a round staging area where the baristas created drinks and the kitchen delivered food.

The café was quiet, with students getting in some late-night studying while others read or checked their phones. Shawn loved Think Coffee because it was spacious, and he could always hide in a corner with his earplugs and shut out the world. He also liked how passionate they were about their coffee and causes. Cheerful signs posted around the café boasted about their fair-trade coffee beans and general love of java. Also, his brother Colin worked there and was speedy about refilling Shawn's Gegarang coffee, his favorite.

Whenever Shawn visited at the end of the day, Colin always had a few colorful stories to share, such as the one about the older man who undressed in the bathroom and stood there until a customer opened the door and shrieked. It was Colin's job to tell the man to leave, and while he did, a young lady opened the emergency exit on the other side of the coffee shop, thinking that it was the bathroom. The alarm blared throughout the café, and people couldn't help but laugh while she hid her face, and the old man paraded through the tables without any clothes or embarrassment. Drugs had numbed that side of him.

The café had been a shady nightclub before Think Coffee took it over. The only reminder of its former days was that very restroom with its dark mini tiles and large mirrors covered with graffiti. Colin told Shawn the entire basement used to be crammed with bathrooms, but

Shawn couldn't understand why they needed so many places to pee.

Violet excused herself to the graffiti bathroom after they arrived while Shawn filled Colin in on all the details of their dates. All four of them.

"You can't have four dates in the same night," Colin said. "That's just one long date."

"We've done something different after each audition. They all count."

"It's your life," Colin said. "I just think it's weird she would schedule so many auditions in the middle of your date."

"Dates," Shawn said, thrusting his chest out.

Colin groaned as he wiped off the table. "Whatever. I thought actors audition during the day."

"I don't know a lot about that world," Shawn said, "but I'm learning."

"I'll bring you both coffees so you can go on date number five."

"Thanks, brother."

Colin made his way behind the barista bar, shaking his head.

After a while, Violet returned to the table. "You know someone here," she said.

Shawn beamed. "I sure do."

"Whenever I saw this coffee shop, I always felt a little intimidated to go inside with a name like 'Think.' I guess I wasn't *thinking*." She smiled at her own joke.

"Are you being funny?" Shawn asked.

Violet frowned. "Obviously not." She checked her phone—no texts from Anton.

Colin brought them two cups of coffee. Violet noticed him checking out her skimpy outfit concealed inside her long coat. She promptly closed it.

"Shawn is obsessed with Gegarang coffee," Colin said, placing the cups on the table. "And apparently with you too." He grins. "Shawn says you're an actress." Violet nodded, hoping Colin wouldn't stay around very long. "What kind of actress are you?" Colin asked.

Violet buttoned the top of her coat. "You know, the basic kind."

She thought that would be enough for him to go away, but he kept staring at her. She searched for something else to discuss. "How long have you two been friends?"

Shawn smiled. "Colin is my brother."

Violet sat up a little straighter and bumped the table, which spilled some of her coffee. "Oh, sorry."

"I got that," Colin said as he pulled a towel out of his brown apron. As he wiped it off, he leaned a little closer to Violet. "People say I'm a very protective brother."

"Who says that?" Shawn asked.

Colin glared at him. "You know. People."

The room started to feel like it was caving in on Violet. She checked her phone. "Didn't realize it was so late."

"We just got here," Shawn said, taking a sip of his coffee. "And this'll give us the energy to go on another date."

"Another date?" Violet asked.

"See?" Colin said.

Shawn took out his wallet and put one of his credit cards on the table next to Violet's purse. "Colin, it looks like we'll be going."

"It's on me, bro," Colin said.

Violet picked up her purse. "No, I need to be going. It's been a long night."

"I want to see you again," Shawn said, and then he looked away as if he were getting ready to be let down.

Violet couldn't make any promises. Not with her life. "Yeah, we'll see."

Shawn started tearing his napkin into tiny pieces. Colin shook his head as if he'd seen this before. "It'll be okay, bro. Let her have some space."

Standing up, Shawn faced Violet. "I really like you."

Violet's eyes widened. She wasn't used to someone talking to her like this. "You barely know me."

"I know you're five-eight. You like sugary cereal as long as your mom didn't like it, and acting, and muffins, and eating enemies for breakfast, if you could," Shawn said with a crisp nod.

Violet's face softened. She squeezed her eyes shut and asked herself what she wanted next. That wasn't something she got to ask very often. "I'll call you."

"The last time someone told me that, I waited a long time. And my phone never rang," Shawn said, staring at his hands.

Violet knew she would never talk to this man again. New York was a big city, so there was little chance they would run into each other either, especially in her world. "I will. I promise."

"Really?" Shawn asked, rocking on his feet.

"Sure. Have a great night," Violet told him sweetly. She turned to Colin and tried not to say anything to blow his impression of her. "Good to meet you, too."

Colin's eyes narrowed on her as he faintly smiled and said, "Goodbye." As she left the coffee shop, she tried not to think of her next appointment.

The key to Violet making it through her nights was taking her happy pills and putting her mind somewhere else while she put what she learned in high school drama class to work. She'd tell them what she thought they'd want to hear while clutching the sheets and thinking about something she saw on television, ways she could rearrange her apartment or her favorite brownie recipe. 1/2 cup butter, 1 cup sugar, and 2 eggs. "You're such a stud!" One teaspoon vanilla extract, 1/3 cup cocoa powder, 1/2 cup flour, 1/4 teaspoon baking powder. "Come on, yeah." Preheat oven to 350. Melt the butter. Stir in sugar, eggs, and vanilla. Beat in the rest. "Oh, you're amazing!" Bake in the oven for 25 minutes.

Sometimes, the john would want to stare into her eyes as if they were both experiencing something real. That made her cringe. She'd force herself to stare right back at him, though, since that would make it less likely he'd hit her. But she would analyze why his head was shaped the way it was or try to figure out what he had to eat for dinner, which was often obvious.

More times than not, the johns wanted her to leave without saying anything. They were finished with her. What was the point? Sometimes the johns would go into a tirade, yelling at Violet about what a terrible person she was for what she did or slapping her around. Her best strategy was not to resist. That just made things worse. She just kept her head down and apologized until they regained control of themselves.

She tried not to take the insults personally. Still, it was a challenge to keep out all the words they yelled. Now and then, a few sunk in and cut at her. The worst clients were the ones who droned on about why they were with her. "I like being the boss," one of them said to her as he pulled back her hair so tight, she wanted to scream. "You don't make me explain why I want to do anything. You never tell me you're tired or you don't feel like it. You do what I say, no matter what. That's a powerful drug." Then he punched her, and she blacked out. Anton made him pay extra for that night.

One of her johns called her "Emily" and pretended she was his coworker. "Emily wouldn't give me the time of day," he said to Violet as he zipped up his pants. "I'd rape her if I knew I could get away with it." He threw a few extra twenties her way. "You're the next best thing."

The pills were the biggest help in getting her through the nights, though their effects seemed to be diminishing. Sometimes she'd fantasize about downing the entire bottle at once. That would stop all the pain for good.

Back in the coffee shop, Shawn glowed. "I set some new records tonight."

Colin picked up their coffee cups. "She doesn't give me a good vibe."

Shawn lowered his head. "Please don't say that."

"It's always good to keep your options open," Colin said with a shrug.

"My options are running out. I bet Dad would like her."

Colin laughed. "Who cares what Dad likes?"

Shawn looked down to the ground. "I was thinking of calling him."

Colin sat on the chair, facing him. "Bro, you can't do that. Grandma is our only family now. Mom and Dad gave us up long ago."

"They didn't give us up. They just didn't like taking me into Manhattan for all my appointments. My autism was too much for them."

"That was just their excuse."

"I wouldn't talk to them or look in their eyes. When they tried to hug me, I'd push them away."

"Yeah, and you were two years old. Stop fixating on that. If it weren't for Grandma and Grandpa, you wouldn't be where you are today. At least they didn't give up on you."

Shawn nodded. "They paid a lot of money for my treatment."

"Mom and Dad only wanted to blame us for their crumbled marriage."

"But it got better after we moved in with our grandparents," Shawn said.

Colin got to his feet. "Of course it did. Because they could get back to what they did best. Making everything about each other."

"I still think they must think about us now and then."

"They know where we live. If either of our parents cared, they'd visit without their breath smelling like alcohol. We're better off without them." Colin looked Shawn over as if he were considering something. "You know, Grandma has always bugged me to help you find someone. Maybe it's time I did."

"I like Violet," Shawn said, hunching over.

"I don't think she's the settling down type. I'll help you find the right kind of girl. We'll start with this," Colin said, motioning to Shawn's polo shirt.

"These are better clothes?" Shawn asked Colin as they made their way through the Nordstrom store on 57th Street and Broadway.

Persian rugs covered the floor, a tiled ceiling loomed overhead, and antique furniture was placed next to the shiny steel and glass fixtures that housed different clothing. Several video monitors displayed colorful pictures of trees and leaves, but Shawn avoided looking at them because he knew he'd get lost in all those colors. Shawn could never go into a store like this alone. The colors, patterns, and music would drown him out before he even made it to a shelf of jeans that were made to look like they were worn before they were.

Colin combed through the carefully displayed clothes on the glass shelves as Shawn trailed him. "I'm telling you; women want you to look like you care about looking good, but not so good they think you're going to compete for counter space in the bathroom."

"I don't like having anything on the counter."

"Say goodbye to the days of looking like Grandma dresses you," Colin said with a knowing grin.

"She's a big help. What's wrong with that?"

"Nothing, if you're five. But most of us don't wear the same thing every day." Colin grabbed a few more pairs of jeans while a salesperson in his twenties wearing ripped denim and a man bun glanced over.

"I mix up the colors," Shawn said.

"You dress like a Lego. Time to dress like a man." They approached a row of mannequin legs hanging from a shelf, dressed in denim. Colin picked out a few more options.

Shawn rubbed the back of his neck. "I'll forget how to match everything up."

Colin groaned. "We'll take pictures. And maybe we can shape up your hair a bit too."

Shawn checked his phone. "That's the millionth time you've checked your phone," Colin said.

"She hasn't texted or called me."

"Once I'm done with you, you won't even care." Colin carried a pile of trendy clothes and motioned Shawn toward the back of the floor.

"Let me know if you need help," the man bun salesman said as he opened one of the fitting rooms.

"We've got this," Colin said. He picked out an ensemble and

directed Shawn to try it on. As he was squeezing into the jeans, his phone rang. He didn't recognize the number but hoped it would be Violet.

"Is this Shawn Lambent?" the voice asked.

"Yes."

It was an agent from the fraud detection department from one of his credit cards. "Have you made large purchases at Meg?" the agent asked.

"Is that a person?"

"It's a clothing store in Manhattan," the agent said.

Shawn pulled out his wallet and realized one of his credit cards was missing. The same one he took out of his wallet at Think Coffee. Shawn must've left it behind. "That wasn't me," he said. The agent explained how they would be canceling his card and sending him another. Shawn vowed to be more careful before hanging up.

"Everything okay?" Colin asked.

"Yeah. Someone used my credit card at a place called Meg boutique. I think it was some kind of accident." Shawn didn't want to say anything else. He didn't like it when Colin used those moments to remind him that he needed to be more responsible. He had his grandma for those reminders.

Shawn inspected his reflection in the three adjoining mirrors outside the fitting room, wearing a dark blue shirt with a white crisscross pattern, jeans with a few worn spots here and there, and a brown leather jacket. He looked good. Handsome, but approachable. *Not bad.* Colin coiffed Shawn's hair and made him look even more styled.

"Well?" Colin asked him.

Shawn nodded to Colin and smiled. He felt taller and stronger, like he could take on the world, and he loved that Colin was spending all this time with him. Since Colin moved out of Grandma's apartment shortly after Grandpa's funeral, Shawn rarely saw him outside of the coffee shop. Colin explained his move as an opportunity for him to live in the now hip Bushwick area, but one night before dinner, Shawn overheard Grandma telling Colin he needed to find a new place to live.

They didn't talk to each other during that entire meal.

Shawn missed having his brother around. Instead of coming home to discover Colin sneaking friends into their room, he was now interrupting his grandma's bridge game or one of her tea parties. Her friends always talked in hushed tones until he stepped into the living room. Then the conversation would get louder and involve something about the Bible. Several of those friends had been coming over to check in on Ruth since her trip to the hospital. Too many visitors made Ruth grumpy. Not enough visitors made her even grumpier.

Shawn looked down at the price tags and winced. "Don't tell me you can't afford it. You never spend money on anything," Colin said. He had a point. This was one way Shawn could invest in his future. Colin had Shawn try on different clothing combinations and took pictures of each. Shawn felt like he was posing for a magazine cover.

"I'm texting these to you," Colin said. "When you get dressed, just match yourself to one of these pictures." Shawn examined the pictures with newfound confidence. That was something he could do. Now, if Violet would only reach out to him, everything would work out perfectly.

# CHAPTER 7

## KEY SOMEONE ELSE

Ruth felt well enough to venture to church on Sunday. She waited for him next to the front door in a vintage dress with her hair done, carrying her coat on her arm.

"Shawn? I know you don't like church starting without us," Ruth said, checking her watch.

Shawn stepped out of his room and walked down the hall, looking snappy in a new ensemble.

Ruth eyed him over. Shawn couldn't tell what was on her mind. Since facial expressions didn't register with him, he needed people to describe what they were thinking.

"Do you like it?" Shawn asked.

"I thought Sunday was red shirt day," Ruth said.

Shawn pressed down his shirt. "Colin says this is better."

"Colin says a lot of things."

"Are you feeling okay?" Shawn asked her.

"I checked my levels, and I'm fine. Did you ever hear back from your date?"

He shook his head. He felt so hopeful when he had parted ways with Violet. But each day that passed drained a little more of that hope out of his heart. Last night, he had decided to join a few new dating apps to make himself feel better, and now he was waiting on a truckload of women to agree to a date. Throughout the night, he had sent a few more texts to Violet in case that would make a difference.

"I'm sorry about that," Ruth said. "You know, sometimes we need a little encouragement, so we don't give up on love." She placed something small in his hand. Shawn slowly opened his palm to discover a sparkling gold engagement ring and a gold wedding band. He marveled at them.

"Doesn't feel right for me to wear them anymore. And I know Grandpa would want you to have them."

"Not Colin?"

"You were at Grandpa's funeral. Colin was at the Comedy Cellar."

"He thought that was the best way to honor him." Shawn's hand flew to his chest. "Is this because you're dying?"

"No," she said, irked. "It's for when you find that special someone someday."

Shawn gave a deep, satisfied sigh. "Thanks so much, Grandma."

She instinctively moved in for a hug but then held herself back, knowing better. She opened the door instead, and they stepped out of the apartment and walked toward the elevator. "Your grandpa would be so happy to know you have those rings. The night before he fell asleep and didn't wake up, I asked him how he felt. 'Handsome,' he told me."

"I don't understand," Shawn said as they stepped into the elevator.

"Grandpa was reminding me of our very first date on a wintry New York evening. After we got our chili, I asked Greg to 'hand some' salt to me. He looked at me with a twinkle in his eyes and said, 'You called me handsome.' I laughed and knew we had a future together."

"If I see Violet again, I'll be sure to ask for some salt."

Ruth smiled as they left the elevator and walked through the lobby, where Douglas, the doorman, hung up his phone. Shawn couldn't take his eyes off the rings, thinking about the day he would slip them onto his wife's finger.

Ruth held out her hand to get them back. "I'll put them inside your desk when we get home. For safekeeping."

Shawn stalled for a moment, took a hesitant step toward her, and surrendered them with a pained look.

Douglas motioned to the street. "Your taxi will be here soon."

"Thanks, Douglas," Ruth said. She opened her purse and tucked the rings inside. "Did you ask about her family?" she asked. Shawn shook his head.

"Her job?"

"She's an actress."

Ruth's face wrinkled with disappointment. "What about her church?"

Shawn shifted uncomfortably. "Not yet."

Ruth rolled her eyes. "You've got to read the sell sheet before you buy the house."

"I'm not buying a house. And I don't even know if she'll call me back," Shawn said, his arms hanging with defeat.

"If she doesn't, she's obviously not worth it." Ruth struggled to put her coat on.

Douglas stepped over. "May I?" Before Ruth could say no, Douglas helped her slip into her coat. "Glad you're doing well," he said with a wink. His hand brushed hers, and she could feel her pulse quicken. Douglas had been a soothing presence ever since her husband passed away. He was the first to not just offer help but actually give it. There were many things around her home Grandpa regularly fixed, often without Ruth even knowing. But when Ruth allowed Douglas to step in as her handyman, it made her feel like she was cheating on her husband somehow. Eventually, she was able to put those feelings aside.

Their fix-it dates progressed into secret walking dates. Ruth would describe to Douglas what it was like growing up on the upper west side, and Douglas shared stories about childhood in Harlem. If she recognized someone from the building walking by them, Ruth would stiffen and talk to Douglas as though they were reviewing official business for the homeowner's association.

Shawn didn't seem to notice the moment between Ruth and Douglas, which was not surprising. The taxi pulled up outside.

"We need to get going," Ruth said.

Douglas handed her a small box. "Package for you." Ruth's eyes flickered with delight for the briefest of moments, then she was back to business as she waited for him to open the door.

The taxi whisked them through the light Sunday morning traffic until they arrived at Redeemer Westside Church on West 83rd Street. Ruth and Shawn emerged from the cab in front of the brick building where people flooded inside through the open glass doors.

Ruth noticed a group of women standing around near the street corner. They looked like hookers. Or drug addicts. Or both. There was something sad and used about their clothes, their makeup, their skin. She winced and kept Shawn moving toward the doors.

Inside the auditorium, Shawn sat next to his grandma in one of the front rows. A small choir tenderly sang, "Turn your eyes upon Jesus. Look full in His wonderful face. And the things of earth will grow strangely dim, in the light of His glory and grace," while a graceful woman led from a piano on the stage.

Shawn gazed at the backlit multicolored stained-glass panels in the shape of a cross hanging behind the choir. As Shawn peered closer at the colors, they seemed to come alive to the music. Each color pulsated with the melody and added sweet-sounding layers to the music. He closed his eyes and prayed, *God, please bring me that special someone soon. Before Grandma dies. I'm worried about her and the future. It would be nice if that someone was Violet. Amen.*

A lanky gray-haired pastor in a tweed jacket talked with passion from the stage. "When we do what we know isn't right, most of us think God doesn't love us. But we can't earn his love by how good we are. Jesus loves us no matter what, even though we don't deserve it. That's God's grace. And that's the kind of love that changes us."

After the service ended, Ruth and Shawn took the elevator to the next floor for the after-church social featuring mini-muffins, orange juice, and coffee. Ruth caught up with some of her friends. Shawn scanned the room for date prospects, until he remembered Ruth's warning. She had told him not to treat church like a meat market. Then she had to explain she meant he should be there for the right reasons, not for the right woman. The right woman would come along when he had the right reasons, she told him. Shawn said he would try to keep his priorities in order, but he had a future to think about. People huddled in conversations around the room, and all Shawn could think about was how great it would be if Violet visited his church with him.

Shawn walked into Think Coffee on Friday, with his shoulders drooping even lower than usual.

"By the way you look, I'm guessing you didn't hear back from her," Colin said to Shawn.

"I might be texting her too much," Shawn said. "Today, I asked her if she heard of that Meg boutique where that person used my credit card. I'm running out of things to say. It's hard to have a one-way conversation."

"You might want to give it a rest. If you're free tonight, I'll get us tickets to a lock and key mixer," Colin said.

"I don't know what that is, but it sounds wrong."

"The women wear a lock on a necklace, and you get a key. Once you open someone's lock, you get to enter a raffle to win prizes," Colin said.

"I don't care about prizes."

Colin smirked. "It's just an excuse to meet the ladies."

"I just care about meeting them."

"Right. And you'd have a reason. Makes it less awkward," Colin said with a shrug.

"Sticking my key in a woman's lock sounds very awkward."

Colin groaned. "It's a step forward."

"Fine. But I'm inviting Violet."

Shawn raced home to dress in one of Colin's ensembles. Then he hopped onto the subway and met his brother at Gallaghers Steakhouse on 52nd Street. As he stepped inside, he noticed the tones of the restaurant were very muted; no colors were going to shout at him here, except the red and white striped window valances. The chandeliers cast subdued lighting across the wood-paneled walls. A well-dressed crowd in their twenties and thirties laughed and conversed as they mingled throughout the room, trying to match keys to the locks women wore around their necks.

Colin handed their tickets to a woman in a shimmering gold blouse who stood at the entrance to the private room. "Don't be shy now," the woman said as she handed them both keys. "You just might unlock your futures. Or you could win some prizes."

"I'll be happy with a date," Shawn said, and the woman nodded. They made their way through the room and settled into a spot next to a round bar area. Shawn peered at all the dangling locks around the women's necks and felt his mouth go dry.

"I'll get drinks," Colin said. He stepped up to the bar and motioned to the bartender.

A pretty woman in her twenties with a faint mustache smiled at Shawn and approached him. He pointed to her mouth and said, "I've seen a device advertised on TV for that."

"Excuse me?" the woman asked.

"You can get that lasered right off."

The woman touched her lip. "Didn't think it was so obvious."

"Anyone can see it's a mustache. But you can fix it in no time," Shawn said with a smile.

Shawn couldn't tell she looked like she was about to cry. Colin was suddenly next to them. "Excuse my brother. He can be a little blunt sometimes."

"Did I say something hurtful?"

"Try your key, Shawn," Colin said, motioning to the woman. Shawn held up his key, but the woman held her hand over her lock.

"Oh, come on. Let him try." Colin looked at her with puppy dog eyes. "Please." She clenched her hand over the keyhole. "It'll take two seconds."

"Key someone else," she said as she fled to the other side of the room. Shawn looked around, wringing his hands. The conversations in the room blended and rose in volume. All he could do was put his hands over his ears.

"Just try a few locks," Colin said, motioning to a group of women nearby. Shawn looked back at him with wide eyes. Colin groaned.

"Can I try?"

Colin turned to see Violet standing there, her coat closed tightly around her. She held up her apartment key.

Shawn's face lit up. "You're here!" He turned to Colin. "I told her to stop by between her auditions."

"Can we talk for a second?" Violet asked, motioning Shawn over.

"Sure," Shawn stepped over with a smile on his face that made him look like he'd just won the lottery.

Violet talked in a hushed tone. "I got your texts. And the one about the boutique. Tell me how you wanna work this out."

Shawn furrowed his brow. "Work what out?"

Violet pulled Shawn's credit card out of her pocket and handed it to him. "You had this?" he asked.

"I thought that's why you texted me."

"I was hoping you wanted to see me again."

She peered at him closer, unsure of what to do. She came here thinking he had caught her and would tell her what she had to do to make up for it. But this was entirely different. "I must've grabbed it when I left the coffee shop. It was a stupid mistake. I returned all the clothes. Sorry about that."

"That explains it," Shawn said, taking the card.

Violet looked him over. "Nice look."

Colin stepped over, motioning to Violet. "Can I chat with you for a moment?"

Violet nodded, and Colin pulled her aside, out of Shawn's earshot. "What's going on?" he asked her.

"Your brother is very unique."

"He's autistic." Violet looked back at him with a confused look. Colin continued, "He's high functioning, but it's tough for him to form relationships, communicate, read social cues."

Violet snickered, "I might be that too."

"He can be too trusting, too loyal, and when he hurts, he hurts big time. And he isn't loaded. Did you think he was?"

Violet put her hands on her hips and could feel her temperature rising. "Why would I think—"

"I know how the world works," Colin said, cocking his head. "Are you really an actress?"

Violet's face reddened. She didn't like being grilled like this. "That's why I moved here. To get my big break," she said sincerely.

"He deserves a nice woman. No offense, but I don't think you're his type."

Violet's anger boiled inside of her. *How does he know my type? How can he tell I'm not nice?* She was used to overhearing people talking about her in the streets or in the lobby of a hotel, but this guy was looking right in her face. She huffed. "The only time people say, 'no offense' is when they know they're going to say something offensive."

"I didn't mean—"

"I know what you meant," she said with hard eyes. Violet turned toward Shawn. The way he looked at her—it was so earnest, it was painful. She wasn't going to let him go. Not tonight. Not with his brother breathing down her neck. "Wanna get something to eat, Shawn?" she asked.

Shawn nodded, bouncing on his toes. "The only lock I care about is yours."

"Well, you're in luck because it's wide open." She glided past Colin and took Shawn's arm. He shook her off, but she stood beside him as though his reaction was perfectly normal.

"Let's go to a quieter area of town," Shawn said to Violet.

"Sounds good to me."

Shawn handed Colin his key. Before they stepped outside, Violet shot Colin a defiant glare.

# CHAPTER 8

## A DIFFERENT WAVELENGTH

Shawn and Violet strolled across to the 50th Street subway station, where they took the E train down to the village. They navigated through the weekend crowds until they arrived at Washington Square Park. The air was sweet with the smell of honey-roasted peanuts cooking in a stand at the edge of the park. They stopped to listen to a pudgy man with a droopy mustache. He sang a folk song and strummed his guitar beneath the marble Washington Square Arch that towered overhead. Shawn dropped a few dollars into the musician's open guitar case.

"This place used to be farmland. The government gave it to ex-slaves in the late 1600s and told them their children would be born as slaves even though they should've been free," Shawn said.

"Guess the world has never been fair."

"Then it became a public burial ground. The remains of over 20,000 people are buried under our feet."

"It's a pretty place to be stuck underground."

They ventured down MacDougal Street, past La Lanterna di Vittorio, a small cafe. "My brother used to work there," Shawn said.

"That's the closest I've gotten to Italy."

They passed the bright bulbs of the Comedy Cellar and turned onto Bleecker Street, where they wandered by a storefront filled with racks of wedding dresses. Shawn lingered in front of the window for a moment before they continued. Then he kept glancing at his phone.

"Maybe I can help you find a place to eat," Violet said.

Shawn handed her his phone. She looked at the screen that glowed with pictures of smiling brides and grooms.

"These aren't restaurants," Violet said.

"That's one of my favorite wedding sites."

"Oh yeah?" Violet cleared her throat. The phone suddenly felt heavy to her.

Shawn walked with a skip in his step. "It lists what you need to do a year ahead, eight months ahead, all the way down to the big day. With checkboxes. You can see some of my other favorite sites if you swipe your finger."

She swiped across the screen, not sure why she was walking through Greenwich Village with a guy she barely knew, looking at websites about getting ready for your big day. She peered at links to articles about *How to Give the Best, Best Man Speech, Fancy Invites with a Simple Budget,* and *What Wedding Colors Say About You.* Shawn glanced at them over her shoulder, with a look of delight in his eyes.

"I know a guy who posted an ad that said wife wanted," Shawn said.

"Yeah?"

"He got a bunch of replies that said, 'You can have mine.'" Shawn peered at her with a grin, as if he thought she was going to laugh. She didn't.

"Is that a joke?" she asked, looking at him sideways.

He nodded. "Colin's better at those. My grandpa was the real jokester in the family."

She handed his phone back to him. "All this walking is making me hungry."

He motioned to his phone. "Inspiring, right?"

Violet flicked her hair back. "I guess."

"Finding a place to eat can be a challenge. I can't eat certain textures," Shawn said. "Or casein, which is in milk and cheese, or gluten, which is part of wheat. We could look for something near your place."

That was precisely what she didn't want to hear. "I'm way out there. East New York."

"I like riding the subway. Especially the empty cars. What's your address? I'll look it up."

She hesitated and shifted her weight from one foot to the other. "1600 Pennsylvania Avenue."

"Seriously?"

She nodded.

Shawn beamed as he entered her address into his phone. "Like the White House."

"Yep. I hear that a lot."

"Do you have a rose garden?"

Violet laughed. "The only thing growing in my part of town is crime."

"Violet!" Her heartbeat quickened at hearing Anton's demanding voice. She looked across 7th Avenue, where he stood in baggy jeans and a hoodie. Anton waved her over.

"Give me a minute," Violet said to Shawn. He nodded, and she raced across the street.

"You got me worried, sweetie, when I didn't hear from you," Anton said as Violet approached.

She could feel her insides knot up. "You didn't have anyone lined up, I thought—"

Anton squeezed her arm. "Let me do the thinking. Did you get my text?"

Violet took out her phone and glanced at the screen. "Looks like it froze."

"I'll get you a shiny new one if that's what you need. Anything for my honey. You're good for it." He gave her one of his menacing smiles.

Violet's hands trembled. "It works. Just a glitch."

Anton glanced across the street. "You with that guy again?"

"Just working him."

Anton leaned forward, and Violet braced herself to be struck. He softly kissed her on her cheek. "When you finish, meet me over by that place near the thing where we went that one time."

Violet nodded. She was never sure which was worse, being hit or kissed. When he beat her, Violet knew she did something wrong or didn't talk to him respectfully. But when he kissed her, it usually meant she was about to have a busier night than usual, or Anton was going to pair Violet with someone who would be especially unlikeable. Anton strutted away, and Violet felt a weight on her chest, thinking about what the night had in store.

Violet waited for an opening in the traffic, then she ran back across the street to Shawn. "Sorry. Thought I was free tonight." With a shaking hand, she opened her purse and reached for the one thing that made her nights bearable. She popped open her pill case and popped one in her mouth.

"Something's wrong with your hand," Shawn said.

"Nerves, okay?" she said, glaring at him. She looked down, and her shoulders drooped. "Sorry I snapped."

Shawn's face softened. "I could never go on auditions. Or act. For anything. You're very brave."

She smirked. "Or crazy." It was hard for her to grasp that he still believed her story, but he did. And she was grateful. It gave her a chance to be with someone who treated her like everyone else before she slid up her walls and lost that sense of normalcy for the rest of the night.

He looked into her eyes. "You're a different wavelength."

Violet tilted her head. "What do you mean?"

Shawn paused to look her over. "There are colors we can't see. Beauty that's outside our visible spectrum. There's a lot about you that's not visible to me yet. But I can tell it's going to be beautiful."

Violet could feel her eyes well up with tears, but she fought them back. She wasn't used to hearing kind words that weren't veiled threats or tools to get her to do something. She couldn't trust people's words.

"Can we try the hug again?" Violet asked. She took a step toward him, but he pulled back. "What if I hug you gently?" She tried to put her arms around him, but he pulled out of her grasp and looked down. She waited for a moment. "Can you give me a hug?"

He looked up. Scooting a little closer to Violet, he carefully put his arms around her. She had never experienced someone come so close without actually touching her.

"You smell like flowers," Shawn said as if it was the perfectly natural thing to say. "That's the best I can do for now."

She unbuttoned the top of her coat, revealing a plastic pink lollipop necklace in the shape of a heart that dangled from a silver chain. "My necklace. How does it sound?"

Shawn gazed at the color and listened. "Like whispers."

Violet's face heated, and her heart pumped harder. She peered into his eyes, but he kept his gaze turned from her. He pulled his arms away and focused on the ground.

She started to embrace him, but stopped, out of consideration. Smiling, she ran her fingers through her hair. "Since you won't let me, I'll just say it. I wanna hug you, Shawn."

Her words hung there for a moment. From the look on Shawn's face and how he fidgeted, he didn't know what to do or say. "And that's not an everyday event for me. I've had a lot more touching than I need." She thought ahead to the next few hours, to the men who would grope her, push her, press into her, suffocate her, or treat her like they owned her.

"I don't know what that means," he said, puzzled.

She took a breath. "I need to go."

Shawn stepped in front of her. "I want to see you again."

Violet struggled to find the right words. "It's just not... I don't think that's going to work out." She clutched her purse to her side and gave him a final nod.

"Please don't say that," Shawn said. "I really, really want to see you again."

Violet smiled tenderly as she made her way past him. "I know."

She waved goodbye and headed up 7th Avenue and. As she walked away from Shawn, she could feel the dark cloud descend upon her. She was used to that cloud impacting her day, but when she was with Shawn, she could sense it was breaking up, and something new and unexpected was beginning to shine through. But even now, their time together felt like a distant memory.

Violet descended the steps into the dimly lit subway tunnel to make her way to the men waiting to invade her.

That Wednesday afternoon was equally cloudy and muggy. Shawn sat next to the front window of Think Coffee, typing away on his computer while Colin wiped off the table next to him.

"I showed Violet my favorite wedding sites," Shawn said, taking a sip of coffee.

Colin grinned. "And she didn't run away screaming?"

Shawn shook his head.

"Grandma called me the other day, which is a rare event," Colin said. "Asked me for details about your love life. She didn't get a good vibe about Violet, either."

"Grandma told me she's suspicious about Violet, but she's suspicious about everyone." Shawn set down his coffee cup. "I finally have a relationship, and you're both against it."

Colin pressed the towel against the table hard as he wiped. "You're too trusting. That's how you get hurt."

Shawn shook his head. "Don't bring up Amanda."

Collin's eyes tightened. "You carried her picture around for years."

"There's nothing wrong with that," Shawn said.

"Oh, no. You still carry it around."

"She meant a lot to me," Shawn reached into his pocket and pulled out a picture of Amanda. She was positioned at a three-quarter angle to the camera, looking over her right shoulder and wearing a rose-colored dress. Cute and freckled, she was eighteen years old with a shock of red hair.

Colin shook his head in disbelief. Shawn returned the picture to its home in his pocket. After Amanda passed away, he promised himself he would always keep her picture close, so he wouldn't forget her.

"See? That's what worries me," Colin said. "It takes you too long to get over someone you care about. I don't think Violet is worth your time."

"She is if it means there's a possible future for us."

"Look at the way she dresses," Colin said. "Makes me think she has a past or something,"

Shawn motioned to three slender ladies in skimpy, tight miniskirts who were ordering at the coffee bar, dressed like they were going out to a club. "Do they have a past?"

"Of course they do. Those girls aren't your type, either. And those auditions at night, what's that about? You think she's really an actress?" Colin furiously cleaned the table.

"That table isn't getting any cleaner." Shawn's face hardened. "At least I'm thinking about my future. You're probably the only barista here with a teaching degree."

Colin held up a hand to ward off Shawn. "Hey. Ouch."

"You could be doing more with your life."

"And you should ask her more questions. Get to know her. Find out what she actually does."

Shawn groaned. "I know what she actually does. Just be happy for me." He slid his computer into his bag.

"I want the best for you," Colin said. "I really do."

Shawn stormed out of the coffee shop, unconvinced. He couldn't figure out how his brother could be so insistent on him finding someone one minute and be so against it when he finally did.

Colin hadn't approved of Amanda at first, either. When Shawn started school at Columbia University, he met Amanda during freshman orientation. Shawn couldn't stop listening to her crimson hair. She invited him to an outing at a jazz club, but he explained to her how it would be too stifling for him to go.

Instead of going to the club without him, Amanda suggested they take a stroll across the quiet Columbia campus that night, and Shawn agreed. He told her about his programming ambitions, and she explained how she wanted to bring medical aid to people in poor countries by getting a nursing degree. When he explained his autism, she told him how much she admired him for not letting that hold him back from anything.

Colin told Shawn that Amanda was dating him as her personal good deed project. So, he invited himself on one of their dates. Amanda smiled warmly when she met Colin, and the conversation quickly turned to Colin's area of expertise—coffee. Colin appreciated her penchant for dark roast and liked her immediately. Then he convinced their grandparents to get on board. None of them ever guessed Shawn's relationship with Amanda would end so tragically.

# CHAPTER 9

## EVERYBODY LIES

Shawn strolled alongside Violet in Central Park at 59th Street, near the horse-drawn carriages that waited patiently for willing tourists. Shawn bought hot dogs from a fast-talking, heavyset street vendor and handed one to Violet. Then they walked along the outer path that wound through the park while joggers and bicyclists whizzed by them. The day was overcast and cold. Violet cinched her coat to conceal her 'working' clothes. Shawn winced as he ate his bun-less hot dog.

"Not a fan of hot dogs, I see," Violet said. "We can get something else."

"It's the texture. I try not to think about it," Shawn said, hoping Violet didn't care. When she agreed to meet up with him again, he was thrilled. He didn't want to do anything to mess up their time together. "Thanks for getting together."

"Oh, I was in the city. Had some time off between auditions."

"Well, I'm always happy to be your escort."

Violet looked up to him, her face tense. "Excuse me?"

"When you go on your auditions. I like going with you."

"Oh. Yeah." She looked around at several joggers speeding past them.

Shawn kicked at a leaf on the ground as they continued down the sidewalk. "Why'd you decide to go into acting?"

"It was always a dream. When I moved here, I didn't get a lot of auditions. Then...my boyfriend showed me how to act." Violet bit her bottom lip.

"What happened to him?" Shawn asked.

"Uh. He's my manager now. Anton. You met him. I borrowed some money. He had me do some favors, some acting, to pay him back." Violet took an uneven step forward and looked around again.

"Are you looking for something?"

"My manager. Let me know if you see him."

"He's meeting you here?"

"The opposite. I'm hoping I don't see him here."

Shawn nodded. "Colin doesn't think you're an actress."

"He doesn't know everything," she said in a flash of anger. She took a breath. "Sorry. He seems very protective."

"It's hard for me to figure him out. He says my grandma doesn't have a good feeling about us either," Shawn said.

"You're an adult. You can choose who you spend time with," Violet said. Shawn looked back at her blankly. "You don't need to tell them everything about what we do."

"I can't lie. I don't like lies. My grandma says everybody lies, but...it doesn't matter, um, since nobody listens."

"Joke?"

He nodded. "Still trying." They passed a young couple arguing.

"I'm not saying to lie, I'm just saying it's good to have choices. You get to decide where you go and who you see, right?"

Shawn nodded.

"Don't take that for granted," Violet said. Her stomach tied into a painful knot. The wind whipped Violet's hair into her hot dog mustard. Shawn grasped her hair and wiped it off with his napkin. Violet was moved by his kindness, by his proximity.

"Every day, my co-workers judge person after person to see which ones should have love. I think the whole reason we exist is so we can be loved," Shawn said.

"It's a nice thought," Violet said flatly. She never liked hearing people say things about love that could only be true inside a greeting card. She knew how the world really worked.

"That's why God created us. So we could be loved." Shawn gave her a hopeful smile. He opened his mouth as if he was about to say more but stopped himself and took a breath.

Violet kept herself from saying something sarcastic. She didn't want to crush the way he saw the world.

"This is probably a good time to tell you about my rule," Shawn said.

Violet raised her eyebrows. "Your rule?"

Shawn touched his fingertips together. "I don't date just to date."

"What do you mean?" Violet asked, rubbing her forehead. An older woman pushed a double stroller with two crying babies past them.

"If I'm dating someone, I see them as a possible wife. If that changes, I stop dating."

Violet grinned. "Have you broken up with a lot of girls over that?"

"Well, no. But I've never gotten this far," Shawn said, thrusting out his chest. "Would you keep dating me if you didn't see us getting married?"

Violet took a moment. She could hear Anton's mocking voice inside her head, telling her he was the only one who would ever have someone used up like her. She hated hearing that but knew it was true. "I don't think everyone should get married."

Shawn looked up to her. "But you want to get married someday..."

"If it's possible." She gazed into his eyes for a moment, and he let her. She wondered how differently he would treat her if he knew the truth about her. Her heartbeat quickened at the thought, but she pushed it out of her mind. She glanced away and dug into her purse. "Almost forgot." She pulled out a black silk bow tie and handed it to him. It was the real kind, not a clip-on. Shawn caressed the silky fabric and treated it like it was made of gold.

"You like talking about weddings and marriage," Violet said. "I saw this at a store and thought you could use it someday. When someone's colors sound right to you."

"A real bow tie. Thank you." He wrapped it around his neck and tried to tie it but couldn't make it work.

Shawn reached out and took her hand. It felt soft and warm. His chest filled with lightness and his pulse quickened. His legs felt weak. He released her hand back to her.

"I should get back to work," Shawn said.

"I gotta go too," Violet said as her face darkened. "Auditions."

"Let me know when I can go with you again," Shawn said.

"I will."

Shawn waved goodbye as he walked away, fiddling with his new bow tie. He glanced back at her one last time with a smile as he kept walking. Violet watched him descend the steps into the subway, and her gaze wandered. She noticed a nicely dressed older couple sitting on a bench nearby, holding each other tightly. The woman nestled her head against the man's chest, and Violet felt an ache deep inside her, in a place she didn't like to feel or admit was even there.

When he returned to his desk at Exclusiv, Shawn glanced over the pictures of the happily married couples taped above his desk. A warm and peaceful feeling bloomed inside of him. Perhaps it was hope. It seemed like now it was only a matter of time before he would have his own smiling wedding picture taped up there too.

Tammy strolled by his desk, wearing a T-shirt that said, *Save Your Mother* with a picture of the earth behind it. "You win the lottery or something?" she asked.

Shawn swatted at a fly. "I don't play the lottery."

"Never seen you smiling this much," Tammy said with a wink. "It's nice."

Shawn gestured to her shirt. "Is your mom okay?"

"It means mother earth. You don't dump garbage in your living room. But we pollute our planet like it's no big deal."

Shawn nodded. "I'll create less trash today if it makes you happy."

Tammy brightened. "Exactly, it starts with you. Now you've got *me* smiling." She continued on while Flynn shook his head.

Shawn's phone buzzed. A text from Violet! *Wanna tag along with me tonight?*

He immediately texted her back. *YES!*

After work, Shawn met Violet outside the Marriott Marquis near Times Square. He followed along with her as she visited different hotels and apartments all over the city.

"I admire your drive to make it," he told her after she emerged from one of those high rises that Shawn called 'Pencil Buildings' because that's what they looked like. "I'm surprised at how many auditions you have to get through."

"Me too," Violet said. "They all blur together."

"You must wonder if it's worth it."

Violet rode to the next audition without saying a word.

Shawn slipped into bed that night and tossed and turned while he tried to fall asleep. Something felt off about the time he spent with Violet that evening, but he didn't know what. As the night had worn on, she became more and more tired until her face looked ashen. Maybe she wasn't cut out for that kind of life. He pulled back his sheets and knelt next to his bed.

"God, please guide my next steps with Violet," he prayed. He climbed back into his bed and finally nodded off.

Shawn stood in a maze of tombstones in the middle of a vast cemetery next to a shiny mahogany coffin. A picture of Ruth stood on an easel next to the casket, beside a black and white painting of New York City. A group of mourners dressed in black huddled near Shawn, crying or hugging one another for comfort. Colin stood nearby, his nose stuck in a book titled, "Funeral Jokes."

Colin looked up and cleared his voice. "When the mortician tried to sell us this casket, we told him it was the last thing Grandma wanted." He waited for a response but got none. He dove back into his book.

A red rose lay at Shawn's feet. He picked it up. The mourners looked up to Shawn as he placed the rose on top of his grandmother's casket. As soon as the rose touched the coffin, the red transformed to black, and the rose dried up and died. Then the whole coffin turned black and started sinking into the ground.

Shawn woke up startled. His heart pounded in his chest as he caught his breath. He quietly stepped down from the bed and walked down the hall to his grandmother's room. Shawn grasped the doorknob and pushed the door open.

Ruth's nightstand lamp spilled a pool of light across her face as she lay back on her bed in her nightgown, with a book across her chest. Shawn took a step closer, his heart thumping. He poked her cheek. Nothing. He lifted her arm and let it drop. No movement. Shawn gasped. This was the end.

Ruth's eyes flickered open as she sat up. "You better have a good reason for interrupting my beauty sleep," she said, wiping her eyes.

"I'm glad my dream wasn't true," Shawn said.

"For your sake, I better be dreaming," Ruth said.

"Thanks for being alive." Shawn smiled. "I never know if today is going to be your day."

"I'm not that old," Ruth said with a sigh. Then she pulled up the covers and motioned for him to leave. Shawn nodded and left her room. Ruth shook her head and turned out her light, sinking back into her bed.

☙

On Saturday night, Shawn carefully studied one of the pictures Colin took of him at Nordstrom and dressed to match it. Once he successfully mirrored the image, he knew it was going to be a good night. Shawn slid his *You're Pulling My Leg!* game book into his backpack along with a few snacks—chips, gluten-free cookies, and apple juice.

In the living room, Ruth sat on the edge of the unforgiving couch, painting a black and white view of Central Park. Shawn pulled a small box out of his backpack as he walked to the front door. "The doorman had this for you. You get a lot of packages."

"Just leave it there." She looked him over. "Big date?"

"I'll be home later," he said, nervous she was going to ask too many questions.

She dipped her brush into the gray paint on her palette. "Is it with that girl?"

"I need to go."

Ruth placed her hands on her hips. "How long did it take you to heal from Amanda?"

"Please don't bring her up," Shawn said, crossing his arms.

"When you get hurt, you're like Humpty Dumpty. We can't put you back together again."

This wasn't the first time Ruth compared Shawn to that oversized egg. After what happened with Amanda, it took some time for him to heal. He still felt an ache from Amanda's absence, especially when he saw someone with red hair or visited a hospital or did something that reminded him of their time together.

Shawn edged closer to the door. "It's getting late."

Ruth raised her voice. "I need her address. So I know where you are."

"I'm an adult. I can make my own decisions."

Ruth narrowed her eyes on him and shook her head, reminding him that he was under her care.

Shawn sighed. "1600 Pennsylvania Ave."

Ruth tapped her foot. "Her real address."

"That's it. It's in the east part of the city."

She scratched her jaw as if she was trying to figure out if she believed him. "What about her last name?"

Shawn could feel his hands get sweaty. "I...I don't know it."

Ruth's forehead creased with concern. "You're going over to her place, and you don't know her last name." She dipped her brush into the black paint on her palette and wore a hard smile on her face. "You're smarter than that."

"I'll ask tonight. You should have friends over for one of your teas."

"I would if it was just the tea, but the conversation turns too quickly to gallstones." She painted a few strokes across the canvas. "At least my paintings make me feel like I have purpose."

Shawn glanced at her work. "I liked them better when they were in color."

Ruth sighed. "Well, this is how life feels now without Grandpa." She looked off into the distance. The love birds chirped. "I still remember him telling me how he knew he was ready to retire. He said instead of lying about his age, he was bragging about it."

"Do you have your medical alert bracelet? In case anything happens?"

Ruth nodded and motioned to her wrist. She didn't want the wristband at first because she said it made her feel old and ridiculous, as though she was in one of those commercials where the woman falls and can't get up. But Shawn and Colin didn't let her say "no" and she finally relented.

"Then have a good night," Shawn said with a smile.

Ruth drew her eyebrows together. "Just promise me you'll call if you feel stuck or anything gets too much for you."

"I'll be fine." Shawn gave her a wave as he made his way out the door and into the chilly evening, on his way to surprise Violet.

# CHAPTER 10

# HER WORLD

After transferring between two trains and a bus, Shawn walked down Pennsylvania Avenue, on his way to Violet's place. Sizable, dull apartments lined the street in this rundown part of Brooklyn where Starbucks hadn't yet opened shop. He approached the entrance to her looming red brick apartment building and scrolled through the names on the directory next to the glass and steel doors. He quickly realized he would need to know Violet's last name to find her among the sea of names. He pulled out his phone and dialed her number. No answer. Maybe this wasn't such a good idea after all.

"You looking for something, sugar?" a woman asked as she stepped out of the building, picking something from her teeth. Her hair was dense and dark with streaks of snowy white, flowing over her shoulders into a tangled mass that spread across the back of her heavy wool coat. At the center of her smile were two gold teeth.

Shawn rubbed the back of his neck. "I'm, ah, looking for Violet."

A smirk snaked across the woman's face. She quickly typed a code into the keypad. The door buzzed, and she opened it for him.

"Apartment 2033," she said with a flutter of her eyelashes. "Have fun."

Shawn stepped through the door and accidentally kicked an empty beer bottle as he walked through the lobby. It rattled across the green-tiled floor. He leaned over and picked it up, thinking he'd put it in the trash. But there was no trash can, so he placed it next to the wall where no one would kick it again.

He pressed the elevator button, but it didn't light up. He pushed it again and again. Nothing. Looking around, he spotted a metal door on the other side of a wall of mailboxes and wondered if it led to the stairs. He started to head over when the elevator dinged, and the doors slid open.

Shawn pressed the button for the twentieth floor and noticed the elevator had a pungent smell. Urine. Perhaps a baby had an accident here. The graffiti-covered elevator groaned as it ascended. It seemed to take forever to arrive on Violet's floor. Shawn walked down the cinder block hallway, past doors where he could hear people arguing, a baby crying, a movie blaring, and someone playing the cello. He finally found Violet's apartment and knocked. Then he waited.

He knocked a second time. Violet cracked the door open, and her eyes widened in surprise. Something looked different about her. Shawn realized she wasn't wearing makeup. She looked clean and pretty, dressed in a loose-fitting T-shirt and jeans.

"Shawn? What are you—"

"You said you like surprises," he said with a wide grin. "I thought we could do a movie night."

"And you found my place," she said, chewing on a fingernail. "Are you a detective?"

"I'm not a detective. A woman out front was nice enough to help me. She had shiny teeth."

"Oh." Violet held onto the door a little tighter. "That was Goldie. She say anything else?"

"Just to have fun. You look pretty."

Violet stared at the floor. "I wish that was true."

Shawn pulled a mini red rose plant out of his bag and handed it to her. She took it, and a smile broke across her face.

"You officially have a rose garden," he said.

Violet smiled smugly. "Now I just need an oval office." She stood there for a moment, looking him over, considering. Then she took a breath and opened her door all the way, welcoming him inside.

Shawn entered Violet's cramped studio apartment. A queen size bed was pushed against the far wall with a worn-out brown couch nearly blocking it from view. A small table and chairs pointed the way to the kitchen at the right of the room, and clutter was everywhere. Shawn's look turned to concern. "Did someone ransack your apartment?"

Violet's cheeks flushed. "No, no. I didn't know we were gonna have company."

A short plastic fence cordoned off an area of the kitchen, where a small brown and white mutt wagged his tail.

"Who's that?" Shawn asked.

"That little trooper is Barney. I found him on the streets."

Shawn reached out to pet Barney who met him with a flurry of wet licks. He pointed to a bandage wrapped around Barney's leg. "What happened to him?"

Violet scratched behind his ears. "A street fight, I think." Violet pulled a bone-shaped treat out of a box next to the stove and fed it to the dog.

"Looks like you're doing a good job taking care of him," Shawn said.

Violet kissed Barney's head. "I do my best."

Shawn noticed several pieces of junk mail on the kitchen table and stacked them into a neat pile. He threw an empty paper towel roll into her trash can and started to wash the dishes in the sink.

Violet fiddled with her necklace. "That's okay, I..." Her voice trailed off as she watched him clean dishes and tidy up. A smile sneaked across her face.

"You live far away from your auditions," Shawn said.

Violet dried off the dishes as Shawn handed them to her. "This is where all the...actresses stay. It's cheap, and our manager likes to keep us together."

Shawn scoffed. "Your manager doesn't have very good taste."

"Tell me about it. Then he keeps most of what I make." Violet put away several of her drinking glasses. Shawn eyed her, concerned. "Welcome to show biz," she said with a shrug.

Whenever Anton gave Violet a cut of the night's cash, it was only enough for her to cover a few necessities. He explained he needed to keep the rest to cover the cost of taking care of her, protecting her, and paying off a debt she owed him from years ago.

A man and a woman shouted at each other from the apartment next door. Violet pounded on the wall—thump, thump, thump. "Give it a rest, will you?" She turned back to Shawn. "Sorry about that."

Shawn pulled out his *You're Pulling My Leg!* book from his backpack, flipped to one of the pages, and read one of the questions, "Tell me about an animal you would be if you could."

Violet put away several plates. "What?"

He motioned to the book. "It's a game inside a book. Helps start conversations. Normally you flip a coin that would tell you if your answer should be true or false. Then I'd vote on if you're telling the truth or pulling my leg. But I'm not so good at that part."

Violet nodded and thought about it for a moment. "I'd be a tiger with wings. So I could fly off and go wherever I'd like but then attack whatever got in my way."

Shawn looked puzzled. "It has to be a real animal."

"You didn't say that."

Shawn returned the book to his backpack and handed Violet a stack of clean forks. "I'd be a basilisk lizard. It can run on top of water."

Violet furrowed her brows. "You said it has to be real."

"It is real," Shawn said, handing her a bunch of spoons to dry. He turned off the water, grabbed a napkin, and started to dust. "It would be an amazing ability to be able to walk on water. Like Jesus did. Except I'd be a lizard."

Violet laughed and noticed he was nearing a bowl of colorful condoms on the end table next to the couch. She hurried over, and discreetly dropped a pillow on top of it.

"What's this?" Shawn asked, picking up an oversized floppy brown teddy bear wearing a purple NYU shirt.

Violet fluffed the pillows on the couch. "That's Theo. Every week, I stuff ten bucks into him. So one day, I can go to acting school at

NYU."

"That's gonna take a lot of stuffing," Shawn said, tilting his head to the side.

"Tell me about it." She fidgeted with her T-shirt. "I know it's a silly dream, but Theo keeps me going."

Shawn noticed lingerie hanging in the closet and darted his eyes away.

"It's just lingerie," Violet said.

"It gets my heart racing," Shawn said, shuffling his feet.

"Nothing wrong with that," she said with a sly smile.

"There is if you're waiting until you're married to make love," he said, shutting the closet door.

Violet laughed heartily. Then she realized he wasn't kidding. "You don't have to wait."

Shawn peered into her eyes. "It's the sign that you're bonded and committed to someone for the rest of your life."

Violet twirled her necklace and sauntered toward him in a joking, seductive way. "Or it's a sign that you like to have a good time."

Shawn rubbed his chin and backed away, looking confused as she swayed her hips toward him. "Are you waiting for that special person?" he asked, blushing.

Violet stopped in mid-stride. Her thoughts raced to how unspecial the men were in her life. There was no waiting with them. They wanted to get down to business fast in whatever way they wanted. Violet always got the sense they were trying to fill up a bottomless pit inside of them, even if it was only for a few fleeting moments. Her face darkened.

"Did I hurt your feelings?" Shawn asked, softening his voice.

"No, I was just—"

Shawn moved closer to her. "I try to ask that if someone's face changes."

"I, um…" She was at a loss for words, not used to someone like Shawn overflowing with innocence and questions. Looking around, she noticed he was starting to get her place in shape. "Maybe you could do this every week."

Shawn nodded with the excitement of a puppy. "I'd love to if I can.

Clutter distracts me." He moved one of her purses over to the dresser next to the bed and noticed a small leather-bound journal. He picked it up and flipped through it. Each page featured simply painted scenes. One page showed a girl in a park, another of a girl ice skating, and another of a girl crying. Violet rushed over and took it out of his hands.

"Not for anyone's eyes," she said.

"Oh, I'm sorry. You like me seeing your underwear, but I can't see your book."

"It's my diary." She tucked it under her arm. "Sorry, I'm not used to someone looking through my stuff."

"I didn't see any words."

"I painted what was going on. Made it harder for my mom to get into my business."

He noticed a picture frame poking out from underneath a blue scarf on her dresser. "Is that private, too?" he asked.

Violet pulled out the picture frame–a photo of herself as a little girl with long hair and an innocent smile, riding a pink and white horse on a carousel. Her parents stood on either side of her. Her mom looked like an older version of Violet, and her dad had salt-and-pepper hair and the chest of a weightlifter.

"That's me when we all went to Hersheypark in Pennsylvania," she said, feeling her face grow warm. "They argued for most of the way down, but I didn't care because we were going to visit Chocolate World."

"That sounds amazing," Shawn said.

"I was so excited to see how they made Reese's Cups and Hershey Bars. A friend told me the tour would end with an all-you-can-eat chocolate buffet."

"I would not do well with that," Shawn said, clutching his stomach.

"You've got nothing to worry about because it didn't. Just a rumor. A sad, tragic rumor."

"You can eat all the chocolate you want now that you're an adult."

Violet smiled. "Yeah, it's just not the same."

Shawn pointed to the picture. "You're cute. So those are your parents."

"This is before Mom kicked me out."

Shawn looked at her with concern. "Why did she kick you out?"

Violet rubbed her hands and looked around. "Oh, long story."

Shawn sat on the edge of her couch. "I'd like to hear it."

"Maybe another time."

Shawn stood back up and noticed another photo on the dresser. This one featured teenage Violet, peeking out through a wall of hair, standing next to her mom, who looked like she had put on some weight. "You're not smiling as big in this one. Where's your dad?"

Violet wrung her hands. "He wasn't with us by then."

"Where was he?"

"He went away," she said, shaking her head, not wanting to go there. She twisted her hair in her fingers.

Shawn held up the two photos side by side and asked, "What happened between these two?"

Violet was non-committal. "Something. I don't know. I try not to think about that."

He set the photos down on the dresser and stepped closer to her. "Why not?" She reached for her pillbox. "Tell me without taking one of those," he said.

Heat flushed through Violet's body, and her face turned red. She gritted her teeth. Who was he, barging in there, asking her all kinds of questions about her life? She pushed her anger down into a place deep inside her where anything that made her feel terrible went to hide. She forced a smile onto her face. "It's not a big deal. Things happen. That's life. People do things they shouldn't. Happens all the time." She could feel her pulse speed up.

Shawn tilted his head to the side. "What did people do?"

Violet could feel her insides start to twist. Her mouth went dry. "It's not like I'm going to see them ever again. Who cares?"

"I care," Shawn said with a low, comforting voice.

Violet glanced up as Shawn moved closer to her. She felt raw and exposed, and she didn't like it. "It was my dad's brother. Whenever he came over, he played with me but not in a good way."

"What do you mean?"

"He touched me, okay? In wrong ways. He told me he'd deny it if I ever said anything and even threatened me. So, I kept it a secret for a long time. When I finally said something, my parents didn't believe me. Thought I was trying to get attention." Holding her stomach, Violet could feel her body tremble as memories flooded back. "My parents started to argue a lot more after that, and I think my mom blamed me for their marriage falling apart. I didn't mind being their scapegoat as long as they stayed together, but it didn't last."

"I'm so sorry," Shawn said.

"After my dad left, I finally stood up to my mom. Then she told me I wasn't welcome to stay with her." Violet wiped an unexpected tear from her cheek. Then she took a breath, pushed down the feelings, and steeled herself.

Shawn carefully put his arm around Violet. But this time, it was his touch that was too much for her. She pulled away. He looked around the room, bewildered, not sure what to do. "That sounds terrible," he said.

"That's how life works," Violet said. "We try to convince ourselves there's a silver lining behind the clouds when there's really just lightning and rain."

"If the sun came out, there would also be a rainbow," Shawn said with a hopeful look.

Violet laughed. "You're not helping."

Shawn motioned to his bag. "Maybe a movie would help? I brought my computer so we could watch one."

Violet shook her head. "Not so fast. It's your turn to tell me something."

Shawn looked at the floor as if he was thinking of what to say. "I didn't grow up with my parents either," he said in a monotone voice.

"How did you get kicked out?" Violet asked with a wink.

"I didn't get kicked out. My parents weren't doing well with their marriage either, and I needed lots of visits with therapists. So, my grandparents took us in," Shawn said. "My parents used to visit us on the weekends. Then they skipped a weekend here and there. Then whole months. Now we haven't seen them in years."

"Sorry about that."

"Thanks. My dad said he needs to find himself before he can take care of us, but my grandma says he'll never find himself at the bottom of a bottle, whatever that means."

Violet nodded. "It was nice of your grandparents to take over."

Shawn pulled a bag of blue tortilla chips from his bag and broke them open. He offered them to Violet, who took a few.

"I almost left them to marry a girl," Shawn said.

Violet raised an eyebrow. "She must've been a special girl."

Shawn hesitated, then popped a chip into his mouth. "Her name was Amanda. She said she wanted to take care of me for the rest of our lives. Then…"

"Then what?

"She died in college."

Violet chuckled. "Wow. I hope you brought a funny movie. We're gonna need it." She looked at Shawn for a smile, but he looked grim. She realized she needed to be serious. "I'm sorry."

"Everyone was sorry when it happened," he said. "We used to meet after our classes to study together. We'd work next to each other for hours. Amanda knew she couldn't interrupt me when I was deep in thought. Sometimes, I would look up and see her staring at me, and she would tell me I was her angel. I told her angels aren't human, and that would make her laugh."

"She really liked you."

Shawn nodded. "When we walked back to my grandparent's place, we'd talk about the future we could have together. Whenever Amanda visited, Ruth taught her how to handle parts of my daily routine so she could do it without anyone's help."

Violet sat on the edge of the couch and motioned for Shawn to sit next to her. "I'm sorry for laughing. Sometimes when things are really serious, that's all I can do."

Shawn slumped onto the couch next to her and looked off into the distance. "She had a defect in her heart that no one knew about. Colin was the one who told me she had collapsed in the lobby of her dorm. They took her to the hospital. I stayed by her side for a week in the ICU, praying for a miracle." Shawn's lips trembled. "The miracle never came." He brushed away a few tears.

"I'm really sorry about that, Shawn." Violet put her arm around him. He stiffened, and she thought maybe that was too much for him, so she pulled away.

"The day of Amanda's funeral, her mom handed me a notecard with Psalm 40:1 written across it. It said, 'I waited patiently for the Lord; He turned to me and heard my cry.' She had found it in her daughter's pocket. That was something we did. Wrote down encouraging verses from the Bible and slid them into each other's backpacks or stuck them in places where we'd discover them the next day. Amanda never had the chance to give that one to me." Shawn turned to Violet. "Most people can get over someone like that in months. For someone like me, it can take years and years."

"Because of the autistic thing?"

Shawn nodded. "But that's not true of everyone who's autistic. Grandma says God gave me a big heart because I'm special, but that sounds like a Hallmark card to me."

Violet's phone buzzed on the kitchen table. She got up from the couch and grabbed it, glancing at the screen. "Looks like I have plans tonight," Violet said with a sigh. "Thank you for telling me your story. I'm sorry I'm not the only one with a dramatic past." She pulled out several nail polish bottles from a basket on her table and returned to the couch. "Whaddya think? Hot pink or mauve?"

Shawn studied her colorful bottles. "I like that one," Shawn said, pointing to a blush red color. She picked it up. "Yeah. That one. It sounds like a heart beating. Or maybe that's mine."

Violet unscrewed the top of the bottle. "You've got good taste."

"You do too. Good night, Violet." He waved to the dog. "Good night, Barney."

Violet talked back to him as the dog. "Good night, Shawn."

Shawn chuckled. He opened the door but then turned back as if he remembered something. "What's your last name?" he asked.

Violet hesitated. "Black."

Shawn raised his eyebrows. "Your name is two colors."

Violet painted her big toe. "You told me black is the absence of color."

"Oh, right." Shawn smiled. "You were listening."

"Thanks for the surprise," Violet said. "I'm looking forward to our next date."

Shawn brightened. "Me too." He opened the door and walked out of Violet's apartment.

Violet stopped painting her nails and sank back into the couch. She let out a breath and wondered how much pain Shawn would experience when he learned the truth about her.

# CHAPTER 11

# AS LONG AS THEY HAVE MUFFINS

Shawn sat hunched over at his desk, typing code into his computer at Exclusiv. He glanced at the pictures of brides and grooms taped above his desk. They were all beaming. Content. He couldn't wait to take his own photos, smiling with the woman who would be by his side for the rest of his life. He now had a pretty good idea who that would be.

He opened his web browser and looked up, "How do I get married in New York City?" He read over the details. Marriage license fee. City Hall. No blood test needed. He was beginning to feel right about this. Getting married was finally starting to feel like reality rather than fantasy.

Tammy passed by Shawn, wearing a shirt that said, "Frack off!" She handed out party passes.

"New party?" Shawn asked.

Tammy approached his desk, relieved she wouldn't have to speed by him this time. "Jake said you could go. Maybe he wants another bet." She handed him a pass, and Shawn looked it over. An art deco style font announced the theme: "Flappers and Gangsters."

"Jake wanted to do Cowboys and Indians until I reminded him how we raped and pillaged their land," Tammy said with an intense look. She took her role as the conscience of the office very seriously.

Shawn returned the invite. "That's okay."

Tammy's eyebrows furrowed. This was not the response she was used to. "I don't like glorifying violence either, but he wants all of us to go. You can bring someone."

Shawn turned away, returning to his computer. "We'll see."

Tammy shrugged and continued onward. Shawn stood up and motioned her back. "Tammy, I'd like to ask you a question about your history rating."

"History rating?" Tammy asked, stopping next to Flynn's desk.

"It's a score we're going to launch that evaluates people's pasts so you know more about the person you might want to date. Jake had me run all the employees through the system."

Tammy returned to Shawn's desk, twisting one of the many rings on her fingers. "Okaaaay."

Shawn tapped on his computer screen where a number four was displayed below a picture of Tammy. "Any idea why your score is so low? Bankruptcies? Anything like that?"

"It's obviously broken," she said with a curt laugh, looking around.

Shawn turned to his computer and scrolled down his list of formulas. "It looks good to me." He looked up, but she was gone. "Tammy?" Shawn glanced around.

Flynn shook his head. "You need more tact, bro."

"Did I say something?" Shawn asked.

"You always say something. That's the problem," Flynn said before returning to his work.

Tammy was handing out the rest of the passes to the other employees as her heartbeat quickened. She could feel her face getting red while she headed toward the entrance.

"Everything okay?" Jake asked as he passed by Tammy while checking his phone.

"Absolutely," she said as she squeezed past him and flung open the glass doors, stepping into the hall. She stumbled down the hallway to the women's restroom and rushed inside, where she splashed water on her face. She clutched her chest. It felt like the air was draining out of the room. She peered at her reflection.

*No one knows*, she told herself. *And they never will.* She decided to take off from work early so she could go visit her favorite vegan bakery. That would make her feel better.

That night, Shawn sat on an overstuffed red chair in the lobby of the trendy Pearl Hotel on 49th Street, wearing a new ensemble with his hair styled. He finally had his look down, and it suited him. Pulling out his phone, Shawn searched for, "How to Tie a Bow Tie," and tried to follow the step-by-step instructions. He couldn't quite get it.

Ding. The elevator doors opened on the other side of the lobby. Violet wandered out, a pained look plastered across her face. She popped a pill, and her shields slid up. Shawn noticed her walking over and stuffed the bow tie into his pocket. He smiled. "How was the audition?"

She clutched her purse and twisted her neck as if it was sore. "It didn't go like I thought."

"You'll do better next time." Shawn said with a smile. He pulled a piece of paper out of his pocket. "I found some more for you."

"What do you mean?" Violet asked, darting her eyes away.

"I created an algorithm to search and document auditions for a female in your age range." He handed her the listings. "You probably know about most of these already."

She looked it over. Listing after listing of roles in films, television, and on stage filled the pages. "Wow. These remind me of when I first got here. I used to go to audition after audition. I'd shape my whole day around where they were located."

"Like you do now."

"Uh huh." As she looked at Shawn, a smile lit up her face. "Thank you, Shawn. I'd love to be going out for parts like these."

Shawn blushed. "Just want you to succeed at this."

Violet peered into his blue eyes and started to say something but stopped when the elevator dinged. A wiry businessman in his forties with a balding head stepped out of the elevator and adjusted his tie. His eyes met Violet's for a moment. Her customer. She could still feel his knee on her back, pushing her into the bed. "I can't breathe," she had screamed to him. But he kept going.

Violet couldn't stand to look at him as he approached. She pulled Shawn in for a hug with everything she had while her heart pounded against her chest. He fought her grip, but Violet held on tight until the man hurried past them. She glanced over Shawn's shoulder to watch him leave through the sliding doors. She pulled back from Shawn and quickly wiped her tears away, which Shawn didn't notice. He was too busy looking through the papers he had printed out for her. It felt like everyone in the lobby was staring at her, even though they weren't.

"It's probably not a good idea for us to see each other on work nights anymore," she said.

Shawn looked up. "Why not?"

"It's tough making it to all my auditions if I always see you in between."

Shawn shuffled his feet. "I didn't know that. I'm sorry."

"No, it's fine. What I do is demanding," Violet said, taking a hesitant step backward.

"You'll get a great role someday," he said with an encouraging smile. Then he motioned to a listing on the piece of paper. "Woman, twenties. Good-looking. Wounded past. Multiple personalities. That could be you."

Violet cleared her throat. "I think it is me."

Shawn looked at her, confused.

"A joke," Violet said, though she didn't feel like it was. She gazed into his eyes again and could tell he was doing everything he could to not look away from her. A warm feeling blossomed deep inside her. *He cares about me. He actually cares about me.*

She tenderly caressed his face. He jerked back, then took a few steps toward her, forcing himself to let her touch him, if only briefly. Violet wasn't used to touching being such a big deal for someone. Most men in Violet's life couldn't wait to press themselves all over her. She appreciated how Shawn was different.

Violet's phone vibrated. She pulled it out and read the screen. "I'm sorry. My next audition."

"You could skip it," Shawn said with a shrug.

"My manager would let me have it if I did." She felt her hands grow clammy.

Shawn gave Violet a long, pained look and then seemed to crumple in on himself.

"If I ignore it, he'll find me," Violet said. "I don't know how he does it, but he always knows exactly where I am."

"Can I see your phone?"

She handed it to him and watched as he clicked on the screen. "What are you doing?" she asked, feeling her heartbeat quicken. She knew she couldn't trick Anton.

"Turning off your GPS." He adjusted her settings and handed it back to her.

"That's how he tracked me?"

He nodded. Violet's phone vibrated again.

"You should turn it off," Shawn said.

She could feel her toes and fingers tingle with fear. "He'd know if I did."

"And he'd stop bothering you."

"He'd bother me even more. He gets scary when he's mad," Violet said, biting her bottom lip.

She recalled a year ago when she ignored Anton's call so she could get a quick nap on a park bench outside of Gramercy Park. When he found her, his nostrils flared, and he kicked the bench inches from Violet's head. She calmed him down by promising to work even later on weekend nights. That became her new normal.

"What kind of food do you like?" Shawn asked.

She thought it over. "Italian."

His smile drooped. "Italian food is all about gluten." He scrolled through restaurant listings on his phone, looking for a restaurant that promised gluten-free options. "I found a place."

Violet gazed into the distance, thinking through what she could say to Anton. *I didn't have good reception. I left my phone in the hotel room. I should get a night off now and then.* She smiled as she imagined the look on his face if she told him any of that. Then she thought about how much pain he'd make her endure. He wouldn't kill her, she knew that much. He'd just take her out of commission for a while until she learned her lesson. She decided not to care. "As long as they have muffins."

They exchanged glances. And laughed.

The cab sped Violet and Shawn downtown to a traditional Italian restaurant on Mulberry Street, in the heart of Little Italy. Geranium plants hung from the wooden rafters. Mandolin music played from a single speaker attached to the exposed brick wall next to the busy kitchen. They shared a tomato and mozzarella appetizer, though Shawn could only eat the tomato. They picked from each other's plates and talked about family moments they wished they could forget.

"There was a Christmas when my dad gave me a leather wallet with blue trim," Shawn said.

"Sounds thoughtful to me."

"It would've been if Colin hadn't given our dad that same wallet for his birthday."

Violet cringed and laughed at the same time. "That's terrible. But not as bad as catching your mom making out with some dude in the back of her crappy car."

"I can't see how that's worse," Shawn said, wrinkling his nose.

"The week before, that same guy asked me to homecoming."

"Ouch," Shawn said. "That's awkward. And I know something about awkward. I've been told I create it all the time."

Violet laughed. "This city is full of awkward. I saw a woman lying across a tipped over newspaper stand eating a pickle. Just like it was the most normal thing in the world."

Shawn grinned. "I saw a mailbox stuffed with fast food. I guess it was hungry."

"Two giant Minnie Mouses were fighting in Times Square. You can't unsee that."

"I saw a couple making out inside a dumpster," Shawn said. "I wanted my eyes to take a shower."

Violet laughed. "This place can be so weird. Last week I walked out of the subway and saw a man holding a sign that said, 'Tell me off for a dollar.'"

"Did you?"

Violet rested her head against her hand. "Honey, I do that for free."
Shawn grinned.

After dinner, they strolled up Broadway and cut across 8th Street,
passing a homeless guy with a beard holding a sign that read, "Will
polka for pasta," which made no sense to Shawn. Violet gave him a
few dollars. They sat on the edge of the fountain in Washington Square
Park and listened to a woman in an electric green sequin skirt and high
heels play the trumpet

She ended her set, and Shawn and Violet made their way to
Magnolia Bakery on Bleecker Street, where they watched the twentysomething bakers layer thick chocolate frosting onto vanilla cupcakes.
Violet devoured a cup of banana pudding while Shawn noshed on a
piece of flourless chocolate cake.

Later, they walked to the subway station on Waverly Place and
passed through the turnstiles, stopping where the tunnels to the
downtown and uptown trains forked away from each other. Violet
waited for Shawn to give her a kiss or a hug or something, but instead,
he waved goodbye as he continued toward the uptown train. For the
first time in a long time, Violet longed for something more.

# CHAPTER 12

## SOMETHING UNEXPECTED

Shawn unbuttoned the top button of his shirt as he paced around his grandmother's living room. It was getting hard to breathe. He raked his hand through his hair, eyeing the front door.

Knock. Knock.

He took a quick breath and opened the door to see Violet standing there in her long gray coat, clearly trying to cover up her skimpy clothes underneath, though Shawn never noticed.

"Where have you been?" Shawn asked.

"I'm sorry. I got tied up," Violet said as she slipped inside. Shawn started to close the door when she stopped him. "Shawn, this is Aleesha and Natasha. They're friends of mine."

Aleesha and Natasha emerged from the hallway. They both looked like they were in their late teens or early twenties; it was hard to tell. Aleesha was tall, Jamaican, and a little overweight, with a plump, happy face. She wore a tight shimmery dress and stiletto heels. Natasha was tall, thin, and Russian. Her hair was straight, her face narrow, and she had dark, intense eyes. She wore a tight lacy red dress and knee-high boots. They glanced around the apartment with wide eyes as they came inside. They walked around carefully as if they were afraid of breaking something.

Shawn stepped closer to Violet and lowered his voice to a whisper. "I thought you and I were having dinner."

"I'll share. It's a cold night, and they were hungry," Violet said.

"You must work a lot to afford a place like this," Aleesha said.

"This is my grandma's place. I do coding," Shawn said.

Aleesha's eyes lit up. "I love coding. Gets me through the day."

"You know how to code?" Shawn asked.

"Oh no, I thought you said codeine," Aleesha said with a smirk.

Violet waved her hands. "Never mind her." Shawn shut the door, locked the security latch, and looked through the peephole. Then he started pacing and wringing his hands. Violet could tell something was off. "Everything okay?"

"My grandma is coming home thinking she's having dinner with just me. You're a surprise. I wanted you two to spend time together. All of you would be too much of a surprise," Shawn said.

"Thanks for the nice welcome," Aleesha said with a hard smile.

"I wish you had told me," Violet said, feeling her mouth go dry. She thought about what she was wearing and pulled the opening of her coat closed all the way. She could feel herself getting hotter.

Shawn straightened out the pillows on the couch. "I didn't want you to get nervous."

Violet could feel her stomach turn to mush. "Now I'm super nervous. We have to do this another time."

"I agree," Shawn said, nodding. Aleesha wiped her finger across the bottom of a painting of a tree. Natasha peered into the birdcage at Cloudy and Sunny. "Are you all actresses?" Shawn asked.

"Yep," Violet said. "Same manager."

Aleesha smiled half-heartedly. "One time, I even had my own Oscar."

"Really?" Shawn asked.

Aleesha blinked at Shawn. "He said that was his name."

Violet rolled her eyes. "She's joking."

"Sometimes it's hard to know when people are tellin' the truth," Aleesha said, nodding to Violet.

"We should go, girls," Violet said.

Shawn grabbed her arm. "Wait."

Violet felt a jolt of pain and jerked away from him.

"What's wrong?" Shawn asked.

Violet motioned to her arm. "Just a little sensitive." She forced a smile onto her face and exchanged glances with Aleesha and Natasha. "I'm fine. Just can't miss an audition again."

Shawn furrowed his eyebrows. "Did your manager hurt you?"

Violet patted down her hair. "He lost his temper, that's all. It happens now and then. He said he was sorry. He just likes us to be professional."

Shawn looked at her with concern. "Doesn't seem right."

"And he smells like onions," Aleesha said, shaking her head.

Natasha snarled. "He thinks they keep him healthy. Try vitamins."

Violet shrugged as though it was no big deal. "I'll be okay. Let's come up with a plan for our special dinner." Violet knew that dinner should never happen, just like this relationship shouldn't be happening. She wanted to tell Shawn the truth so he could move on with his life, and she could return to hers, but something kept her from saying anything. Deep inside her, she wanted to stay with Shawn. He seemed like a light at the end of her long, dark tunnel.

With a click, the top lock on the front door turned and unlocked. Shawn shot Violet a terrified look. The front door opened and hit the security lock. Then it closed again.

Ding dong.

Violet looked between Shawn and the door and snapped into action. She corralled the women down the hallway and into Shawn's bedroom, gently closing the door.

Shawn took a breath. He unlocked the security lock and opened the door to his grandma. She breezed past him, carrying a bag from Zabar's filled with groceries.

"How was the Bible study?" Shawn asked.

"If more women were like the ones in the Bible, the world would be a much better place," Ruth said, carrying the groceries over to the counter.

Shawn eyed the hallway. "Oh yeah?"

Violet pressed her ear against Shawn's door and listened to the murmurs of conversation outside. Aleesha leaned over Shawn's desk and slid open one of the drawers.

"What are you doing?" Violet whispered.

"Anton said you're casing this guy." Aleesha pulled out a few dollar bills.

"Put that back," Violet said, narrowing her eyes.

Natasha held up a checkbook. "Ka-ching."

"Don't blow this for me," Violet said. "I'm in it for the long game."

"Well, I'm not," Aleesha said with a shrug, stuffing the bills inside her dress.

Violet grabbed the checkbook from Natasha. "Where'd you get this?"

Natasha folded a few blank checks in half. "He won't notice a few missing." Violet held out her hand for them. Natasha sighed and turned them over.

Violet's phone buzzed. She took it out of her purse and glanced at the screen. It was Anton. Aleesha's phone buzzed next. Then Natasha's.

"We've gotta get outta here," Aleesha whispered.

"Just give me a second," Violet whispered.

Shawn slid a box of crackers into the cabinet next to the stove. Ruth placed a wedge of aged Gouda cheese in the refrigerator, then stuffed the Zabar bag under the sink.

"I thought I heard something," Ruth said.

Shawn stepped in front of her. "I think the doorman has some packages for you. Let's go down and see."

"I was just there," Ruth said, raising an eyebrow.

"Would you like to go for a walk?" Shawn asked, shuffling his feet.

Ruth crossed her arms. "I thought you were cooking dinner."

Shawn pulled out a bowl from the cabinet and put it next to the stove. "I'm not ready yet."

Ruth tilted her head and studied him as if she knew something was off. "Don't you need my help?"

"I think I've got it."

Ruth smiled. "That would be a first. What are you planning on making?"

"Baked meat thing," Shawn said, blinking his eyes rapidly.

"Baked what?"

Shawn bit his thumb. "I'm forgetting what it's called."

Ruth put her hands on her hips. "The last time you tried cooking on your own, I put out the fire."

Shawn shrugged. "I got distracted."

Ruth pulled a cookbook off the shelf next to the stove. "I'll make sure you don't get distracted again."

Shawn fidgeted and shifted his weight from one leg to the other. "You should leave now," Shawn said, motioning to the front door.

Ruth took a step back. "Don't talk to me like I'm in trouble." She sniffed the air. "I smell bug spray. Or is that perfume? Is something going on?" Shawn avoided her glaring eyes. She looked over at the dining room table set for three people, then back to Shawn. "You're expecting someone."

"Not exactly."

Violet stepped over to Shawn's window and looked down below where the cars looked miniature. They were too far up.

Natasha noticed a few loose dollar bills on his nightstand and discreetly slid them inside the front of her dress.

Aleesha noticed the ant farm on Shawn's desk and picked it up. "What's this?"

"Put it back," Violet said.

Aleesha looked through the plastic casing, at the network of tunnels inside. She gasped. "Something's moving!" She stepped backward, and the ant farm slipped from her fingers.

Something bumped against a wall. Shawn rocked back and forth on his heels. Ruth looked him over with suspicion. "You're hiding something." She marched past him and down the hallway. Shawn ran after her but didn't reach her before she opened his bedroom door.

Ruth's mouth opened wide in shock at seeing Violet, Aleesha, and

Natasha on the floor, sweeping up the sand from the broken ant farm.

"What is going on?" Ruth asked with a shout.

Violet gasped, and the three of them stood up together.

"Hello again," Violet said sheepishly.

Ruth glared at her.

Aleesha brushed off her arms. "Why do white people keep ants for pets? Where I'm from, we kill these little buggers. It ain't right."

"She was looking at your ant farm, and it spilled on her," Violet said. She stomped on a few ants as they scurried across the small piles of sand on the floor.

Shawn laughed nervously. "Grandma, you remember Violet, my girlfriend. These are her friends, Natasha and Aleesha."

Ruth clenched her teeth. "Don't call someone your girlfriend just because you're spending time with her. This is going to be a major exterminator bill. And someone has yet to explain why you're sneaking around back here."

Shawn looked everywhere but into the eyes of his grandma. "I, um…"

"I, what?" Ruth asked.

"I invited her over."

"We have rules," Ruth said. "Didn't you say you like rules?" she asked Violet.

Violet swept some sand off the floor and dumped it into the trash can next to the desk. "I'm sorry about your ants."

"My grandpa gave that to me," Shawn said. "To teach me about productivity."

"That freakiness makes no sense," Aleesha said.

"Is that your real name, Violet?" Ruth asked, still fuming.

"Of course it is, Grandma," Shawn said.

"Is it now?" Ruth asked Violet with piercing eyes.

Violet looked down and wrung her hands. "It's more of a stage name. No one uses their actual name." She closed her eyes and took a breath. "My real name is Olivia."

"Olivia Black. That's pretty," Shawn said.

The last time Violet heard someone use her real name was when she was quickly packing what she could into her green backpack, the one she'd been using since elementary school, just after her mother told her she needed to find another place to live. When she stepped off the Greyhound bus at Port Authority in Manhattan, she also stepped into her new identity.

Violet stomped on another ant.

"I can't wait to discover more about Olivia Black," Ruth said with a strange look of glee.

Violet sensed an empty feeling in the pit of her stomach.

"That's why I wanted you to have dinner together. So you can learn more about each other. Did I tell you Violet wants to study acting at NYU?" Shawn asked. "I've searched NYU's website to figure out how much it costs to go there. It's a lot."

"You've told me that several times." Ruth turned to Violet. "And I've heard about your family too. They sound very colorful."

Shawn grabbed a book from his desk and used it to sweep more sand off the floor. "She hasn't seen them in a while."

"That's a shame. Family is important to Shawn. So is your spiritual life. Are you a follower of Jesus?"

"Uh, yeah," Violet said, not entirely sure what she was talking about. No one had ever asked her that question before, but she noticed Shawn brighten at her response.

"Really? What church do you attend?" Ruth asked, tipping her head to the side.

Violet swallowed. "Church of the…Holy Grail."

Natasha and Aleesha looked back and forth between Ruth and Violet, as if they were watching a tennis match, wondering who would win.

Shawn smiled. "Church of the Holy Grail. That's great. I didn't know."

Ruth folded her arms and lifted a single eyebrow. "Sounds medieval. We should all go to your church this Sunday. That's much better than dinner."

"I would choose dinner. But that's just me," Aleesha said with a laugh.

Violet cleared her throat and took a small step back. "Or maybe I could visit your church."

Ruth shook her head and looked at Violet as if she was enjoying watching her squirm. "Oh no. I want to go to yours. Who's your pastor? Monty Python?"

Shawn beamed. "I'd love Violet to come with us."

Ruth looked her over. Violet could feel her judging eyes. "Fine. But you might want to rethink what you wear."

"She can dress how she wants," Shawn said.

Violet could feel her pulse quicken as her anger welled up inside her. She thought she might hit this fancy old lady if they stayed much longer. Anything to make her shut up. "We should go."

"I'll see you Sunday, Violet," Ruth said in a tone most people would use with a child.

Shawn led Violet, Aleesha, and Natasha to the elevator outside the apartment while Ruth stayed behind to assess the ant damage and search for stragglers.

"It was getting hot in there," Aleesha said.

Violet pushed the elevator button and turned to Shawn. "I'm sorry things got a little crazy."

"We'll make up for it on Sunday," Shawn said.

The more Violet thought about the idea of joining him for church on Sunday, the more she felt like she was suffocating. "Shoot. I just remembered. I'm… I'm busy Sunday."

Shawn gave her a stony look. "You said you could go."

"I know, but I don't belong in a place like that," Violet said, pulling at the collar of her coat.

"I'm sure it's no different from your church. I'll text you the address."

Aleesha glared at Violet. "This ain't right."

Shawn looked over at her. "What's not right?"

Aleesha locked eyes with Violet. "You should've told him."

"Told me what?" Shawn asked.

Violet shook her head and could feel dread creep up her spine. "My real name. I'm sorry. Hardly anyone knows."

Shawn gave her a dismissive shake of his head. "Not to worry. I guess I should start calling you Olivia."

"No, still Violet. Let's stick with Violet." Sweat formed along the hairline on her neck. She pushed the elevator button again.

"At least you got to talk with my grandma some more," Shawn said.

"Yeah." The elevator doors opened, and Violet breathed a sigh of relief. "Good night," she said as she led the women inside. They pressed themselves against the back wall as the doors slid shut.

"See you soon," Shawn said just before the doors closed.

Shawn returned to his bedroom, where his grandma was sweeping the floor.

"Hiding women in your room. What else is going on that I should know about?" Ruth asked.

Shawn sat on the edge of the bed, looking off into the distance. "I'm in love."

"You're in lust. There's a difference."

"No, I really care about her."

"Shawn, just because one of your dates works out for a change doesn't mean she's the one. There are plenty of nice girls at our church you still haven't met. Just be patient. I'm sorry about your ant farm," Ruth said.

Shawn's mind had already gone elsewhere. "It's okay."

Ruth studied him for a moment, then took the broom and left his room. Shawn shut the door and leaned against it, lost in thought. He opened his desk drawer and took out his grandmother's engagement ring, turning it in his hand. He squeezed his eyes closed, picturing Violet in a wedding gown. The sound of the white dress enveloped his mind with a deep, pulsating tone. His body flooded with peace while his thoughts turned to his future. *Is she the one? Yes, I think she is.*

# CHAPTER 13

## THE TOTAL PACKAGE

Shawn typed away on his computer at his workstation while the rest of the office hummed along. He noticed Jake towering over him and pulled out his earplugs.

"Do you need something?" Shawn asked.

Jake presented Shawn with a black cummerbund and grinned in a way that would make most people squirm. "You like that bow tie a whole lot. Thought you could use something to go with it."

Shawn put his hand on his chest and beamed. "Oh. Thanks so much." He took the cummerbund and wrapped it around his waist.

"Nothing to figure out with that one," Jake said. "So now you can spend more time programming and less time trying to be fancy."

"It's for when I'm a groom."

Jake laughed to himself. Then he realized it wasn't a joke. "Are you getting married?"

"Soon, I hope. We'll see." Shawn said with a kind smile.

Jake leaned in close to Shawn. "Let me give you some advice. Love is blind. But marriage? That's an eye opener." He winked at Shawn, who gave him a blank look, and returned to his office.

Shawn scratched his temple and sat back down in his chair. He pulled his bow tie out from his desk drawer and tried to tie it.

Flynn shook his head. He understood why the other employees avoided Shawn; they didn't want to get caught up in a conversation where he dumped a truckload of information on them they only pretended to care about. But he didn't mind as much. Whenever Shawn talked on and on about something he thought Flynn would find exciting but rarely did, Flynn would use those times to think through his upcoming weekend.

Flynn rolled his chair over to Shawn. "Hey, if you'd like to join the app, I'll let you try again."

"That's okay," Shawn said as he pulled on the ends of his bow tie.

Flynn shrugged. "I think it might be good for you."

Shawn looked at Flynn with a gleam in his eye. "I'm in a relationship."

"Oh? That's great," Flynn gave him a tight smile as if he didn't believe Shawn.

Shawn gazed past Flynn. "I think she might be the one."

"That's …that's big news," Flynn said, swallowing. He looked at Shawn with pity and wondered what was actually going on. He returned to his desk and watched Shawn fidget with his bow tie from the corner of his eye.

NYU students crowded Think Coffee, searching for a caffeine jolt to get themselves through the day. Shawn typed away on his laptop in his usual corner spot at the back of the café while Colin took orders behind the counter.

Shawn looked up to see a bookish woman in her forties trying to figure out if she should drop her used napkin through the metal slit for recycled paper, the opening shaped like a wad of trash or the opening shaped like a cup. Colin had explained to Shawn how all three went to the same compost pile in New Jersey, but the customers didn't feel comfortable when there was only one receptacle; they couldn't believe it all ended up at the same place. So, they had to create three different shapes. She decided on the slit.

A tall, lithe woman walked inside, wearing a sleek designer dress In her twenties, she had the classic cheekbones and flowing hair of a model; in fact, she was one. She gestured, cueing Colin. He seemed to know what it meant. "Ready in a flash," he said.

She nodded. "You're the best."

Colin started his coffee creation in the barista area as she slipped the cashier her credit card. Shawn returned to his work, typing in code.

The woman took a seat at a table next to Shawn, sipped her cappuccino, and crossed her delicate ankles. Colin snuck over to Shawn's table and sat down, motioning for Shawn to take out his earplugs.

"Perfect time for you to practice your flirting," Colin whispered, discretely pointing to the woman.

"Trying to finish up something."

"That's Laura King. She's the total package. Just started coming in."

Shawn typed away, ignoring him.

"She's a model. Teaches dance on the side." Shawn shot Colin an uninterested look. "Loves colors. Look how she dresses."

"You should date her."

Colin rubbed his forearms. "I'm just a barista."

"You have a degree. You just need to do something with it."

Colin scoffed. He didn't like being reminded that he wasn't living up to his potential. Even when they were growing up, his grandparents always seemed to notice the progress Shawn was making but not Colin. They probably didn't have enough energy left after helping Shawn. So, Colin started slacking. He found quick ways to make himself look good when they did notice, but eventually, he settled with just getting by.

Shawn reached into his bag and pulled out some stapled pages. "I printed these from the Department of Education website."

Colin read the heading on the first page, "Guide to applying and getting hired." He tossed the papers onto the table and scoffed.

Shawn motioned to his own clothes. "You helped me. Why can't I help you?"

Colin sighed.

"Someone needs to be on your case," Shawn said.

"Stop acting like grandma," Colin said. "You're on thin ice with her, you know."

"No, I don't know."

"Just be careful with your choice of women. If you want to keep living with her."

"She's not going to kick me out."

Colin shot up from his chair. "Don't be so sure." He pulled his towel from his apron, wiped off the table next to them, and then returned to the barista area.

Shawn looked over to Laura. "My brother likes you," he said a little too loudly. Laura raised her eyebrows and glanced over to Colin, whose face flushed red. He ducked behind the counter.

All week, Shawn's thoughts were consumed with Sunday. For a long time, he had thought about what it would be like to walk into a Sunday service with a woman who wasn't his grandma. He could bring her up to the mini muffin reception afterward and introduce her as his girlfriend. *His* girlfriend. It would be amazing.

Sunday took forever to arrive but when it finally did, Shawn got up extra early to give himself time to put his ensemble together. Ruth waited by the front door, dressed and ready to go.

"Shawn? You wanted to get there early. I don't want to keep your friend waiting," Ruth said.

"Girlfriend!" Shawn yelled from his bedroom.

"Maybe your brother could handle you bringing home women like that, but not me."

"I told you I like her, Grandma," Shawn shouted from his room.

"Please, Shawn, I can't stand by as you..." Ruth felt her heart. She started to breathe rapidly. She attempted to speak but couldn't. Her body tensed up and she looked frantically around the room. She headed for a nearby chair next to the sofa and tried to sit but missed the chair. She fell to the floor with a thump.

Shawn heard the noise from his bedroom. "Grandma?" he yelled. No answer.

He ran out of his room and down the hall. His eyes widened at seeing her on the floor. "Grandma?"

Shawn rushed over to her and took her arm. She tried to speak. "It's—It's—" Shawn whipped out his phone.

"It's a panic attack. Tell me everything will be okay," Ruth said.

"You're sure it's not your diabetes?"

She nodded.

Shawn put away his phone. He helped Ruth off the floor and over to the chair next to the couch. "Everything will be okay, Grandma."

Ruth breathed in and out. "I need a minute."

"Everything will be okay."

She squeezed her eyes shut and controlled her breathing. In and out. The lines on Shawn's face deepened with concern. "You're sure it's nothing more? This is how it started with Grandpa."

Ruth grimaced. "You're not helping."

"Everything will be okay. Everything will be okay," Shawn said in a monotone voice.

"You need to mean it." Ruth relaxed into the chair. "I need some water." Shawn rushed to the sink and poured her a glass of water.

"We never know when our time will come," Ruth said.

Shawn fingered the picture of Amanda inside his pocket. He could feel pressure building inside his chest.

Shawn looked out the window. "I hope Violet waits for us."

Ruth shook her head. "Please be sensitive right now."

Shawn knew what that meant—he needed to think about her feelings and stop talking. Leaning against the kitchen counter, he tapped his foot while he waited.

Ruth leaned back in her chair and sipped the water. Shawn checked his watch. He sent a quick text to Violet to let her know they'd be late and hoped she would stick around.

Cloudy and Sunny chirped from their cage in the corner of the room. Shawn reached into the cabinet under their cage and scooped out some food for them from the bag of seeds. He unlocked the door to their cage and poured the seeds into their silver bowl. The birds chirped and jumped around.

"Lovebirds mate for life, you know," Shawn said.

Ruth sighed. "You've reminded me of that fact many times."

"I'd like to have someone dedicated to me for the rest of my life."

"She's out there somewhere," Ruth said.

"She's waiting for us outside the church."

Ruth's brows drew close, and her face tightened. "You need to find someone who doesn't pretend to go to church."

Shawn watched the birds take turns feeding each other, and his heart grew warm. "I wish you'd trust Violet."

"I've been around for a long time," Ruth said. "I know how to judge a book by its cover."

Shawn took a seat on the couch while Ruth flipped through an issue of Architectural Digest. "You seem okay now," Shawn said.

"Let's give it a few more minutes."

"Are you making us late on purpose?"

"Of course not," Ruth said, her face buried in her magazine.

Shawn crossed his arms and leaned back on the couch, checking his phone, so he could count the minutes. He texted Violet again to let her know they were still delayed, but he hoped to be there soon.

After thirty minutes, Ruth texted Douglas about what happened and finally felt ready to go. They took the elevator down and made their way through the lobby toward their waiting cab, past a concerned Douglas.

"I got your text. Are you okay?" Douglas asked.

"Still ticking, but thanks for asking, Douglas," Ruth said.

"What a beautiful day. Wish I had someone to go for a walk with me when I get off at five."

Ruth grinned. "Hmmm. I think you'll find someone."

He handed Ruth a small package. "This arrived."

Ruth pulled a small, rectangular box from her pocket. "And I found this. I think it's yours."

"Isn't that the pen you ordered?" Shawn asked.

Ruth shushed him and felt her face flush.

"Thank you, Mrs. Lambent," Douglas said.

Ruth smiled at him. They hadn't been on one of their walks lately, and she didn't know how to tell him she missed him without feeling like she was betraying Shawn's grandpa. It was a tricky high wire act.

While Ruth's husband, Greg, was still alive, she barely noticed Douglas other than when he opened the door or took in a package for them. Douglas usually didn't work on the weekends, so one night, she asked him what he did on Sundays. Douglas told her he went to a church in Harlem, and she was delighted. Ruth asked him if he'd heard of Showman's Jazz Club on 125th Street, which she and Greg frequented. Not only had Douglas heard about it, but he also had a cousin who had played the trumpet there on more than one occasion. Greg suggested the three of them visit the club together, and that was the beginning of their friendship. When Greg passed on, she returned to the jazz club alone and wept as the music washed over her.

Shawn fixated on the package in Ruth's lap while the yellow cab traveled up Central Park West. "Who sends you all those packages?" Shawn asked.

Ruth glanced out the window. "Don't worry about it."

"Can I open it?" Her eyes tightened and she shook her head. "Please?"

"Fine," Ruth said, handing the package to him. She knew Shawn would keep hounding her and she wasn't in the mood to resist. Shawn carefully opened it, discovering three small tubes of paint in red, yellow, and blue. Ruth released an appreciative sigh. "He knows I haven't painted in color since Grandpa passed away."

"Why is Douglas giving you paint?" Shawn's eyebrows raised, and his eyes went wide. "He's the one sending the packages." Ruth nodded reluctantly. "He must like you," Shawn said.

"They're just little gifts," she said, tucking her hands in her pockets. Her heart fluttered for a moment.

"Why won't you date him?"

"I'm not… We're not… Don't be absurd. At my age, not acting on love is the closest I will ever come to living out my favorite Jane Austen novel."

"Jane Austen?" Shawn's face went blank.

"You wouldn't understand," Ruth said, fiddling with her bracelet. She turned away from him and gazed out the window. A longing to have Douglas by her side swelled up inside of her, but she pushed that feeling down. She wasn't ready.

The cab stopped in front of Redeemer Westside Church. Shawn helped Ruth out of the taxi while he glanced around. "Besides, he's a doorman, Shawn," Ruth said. "How do you think it would look?"

"Why do you care how it looks?" Shawn asked, searching for Violet among the crowd of latecomers entering the church.

"You're the one who hid your girlfriend in your bedroom."

Violet was nowhere to be seen, and the service started twenty minutes ago. Shawn felt like his heart was shrinking.

Ruth shook her head. "Just as I thought. Like oil to water."

"She hasn't texted me back. Maybe she's late too." Shawn's shoulders dropped.

Ruth waved to someone she knew. "She's probably at her church of the Holy Grail. Sitting next to King Arthur."

Shawn furrowed his brow. "She'll show up." He looked at his watch and fidgeted, wiping his forehead. The morning was not going the way he had planned. "Maybe she's inside."

"Her type tends to stay away from the light," Ruth said, tapping her hands together.

Shawn peered at his phone and felt himself losing focus. "She hasn't answered my texts."

"It's better this way, sweetie." Ruth held out her arm. He reluctantly took it, and they continued into the church.

Violet eyed Shawn and Ruth entering the church from a used bookstore across the street, staying out of their view. She was dressed in a simple blue dress and half her usual makeup, pretending to peruse the paperbacks outside the bookstore. Part of her wanted to cross the street and meet up with them. Another part of her told her she had no business going over there.

"How much?" a nearby man with a deep voice asked her.

Violet jumped, and her cheeks flushed. *Am I that obvious?* Her face drained of all its color and her heart shuddered. She cleared her throat. "What?" She turned to face the muscular man who gave her a flinty stare.

"There's no price here," the man said, holding up a book.

Violet caught her breath. "Oh. I'm sorry. I don't work here." She relaxed and suddenly felt stupid. Glancing over at the church again, she debated. She knew if she didn't meet Shawn now, he'd insist she go with him another time. A part of her knew this would not end well. She took a breath and started walking across the street.

# CHAPTER 14

# WHEN COLORS SOUND RIGHT

The lead singer played his guitar and led the congregation as they sang an old hymn set to a contemporary beat, backed up by a keyboardist, bass guitarist, and drummer. Light glimmered through the stained-glass panels hanging at the back of the church's stage, painting colorful specks across the floor.

Violet slipped into the back of the sanctuary and leaned against the wall. She peered over the eclectic crowd and noticed Shawn singing next to his grandma, in one of the front rows.

"I'm sorry. You can't be here," a woman said to Violet.

She looked over to see a sprightly woman with a bobbed haircut trying to escort her away. Violet lowered her head and felt waves of shame wash over her—this was no place for the likes of her.

Violet stepped toward the exit. "You're right. I'm sorry. I didn't mean to..."

"We have to keep this area clear for emergencies," the woman said.

"Oh."

The woman motioned for Violet to follow her. She ushered Violet to a seat at the back of the auditorium. The congregation started singing a new song, and Violet listened to the words.

"Amazing Grace, how sweet the sound. That saved a wretch like me. I once was lost, but now I'm found. Was blind but now I see."

Violet watched the guitar player lead the singing and wondered how everyone knew the words. A teenager next to her with long, jet-black hair moved closer to share her bulletin. Violet smiled at the gesture of acceptance.

It was a muggy day in New Jersey when Violet last visited a church. The heat clung to her like a hot, wet blanket. She sneaked into a large brick church building a few blocks away from her home and waited outside the door marked "Senior Pastor." She hoped the pastor would return to his office after he was done shaking hands with all the well-dressed people she saw filing out the front doors of the chapel. Hopefully before her mom noticed she was missing. Violet had already tried to talk to someone at school, but that didn't go anywhere. She was afraid to speak to the police about her uncle.

The pastor didn't return to his office before Violet's mom marched down the hallway and gave her a quick slap, reminding her that no twelve-year-old should wander off by herself. Her mom asked what she was doing there, but Violet couldn't think of anything to say. She didn't talk for the rest of the day and never stepped into a church building again.

She stopped trying to tell anyone about how her uncle would lie next to her in bed and force her to do things that made her want to crawl out of her skin.

Her uncle used to tell her he loved her, but that needed to be their secret forever. She kept telling herself he would stop, and things would get better the next time her parents invited him over for a visit. But then he'd be back in her bed when everyone was asleep. So, she learned to put her thoughts elsewhere until he was finished. After a while, Violet's body didn't feel like it was hers anymore.

Violet wiped an unexpected tear from her cheek and looked around to see if anyone noticed. She fixed her attention back to the stage and started getting lost in the singing.

Her phone rang.

Violet quickly pulled it out of her pocket and muted it. A few people glanced her way. She checked the screen. It was Anton. *Client waiting. Where r u?* Her shoulders slumped from the weight of it all.

She slowly found the energy to stand up and made her way to the back doors. With a heavy sigh, she took a final look back, and Shawn was suddenly next to her, beaming.

"I didn't see you. We're sitting up front," Shawn said.

Violet pointed to her phone. "I got called in."

Shawn looked baffled. "On a Sunday?"

"I wish I could say no. I like that song. Feels hopeful."

"It's Amazing Grace."

A smile lit up Violet's face. "It really is."

She walked toward the exit, and Shawn followed, wringing his hands.

Violet made her way through the outer doors and over to the curb where she waved for a taxi. Shawn caught up to her. "If we were married, you wouldn't have to worry about money or auditions."

She laughed and thought he was joking.

Shawn shuffled his feet and looked down at the ground. "Is that funny?"

Violet tilted her head. *He isn't joking.* "No, I…"

"Am I someone you would marry?" Shawn asked her with eyes that grew a little wider.

The idea of being hitched to someone for the rest of her life didn't appeal to her. Look how her parent's marriage ended. But here was someone who wanted her and could change her future. *But would he still be here if he knew about the real me?* Violet thought she knew the answer, but there was only one way to find out. "Shawn, I need to tell you something."

He took a step toward her. "Yeah?"

"I never thought we'd get this far. Never thought you or anyone else would bring up…marriage." It felt strange to talk about the "m" word. She mostly thought of her life in one-hour increments, not in years. Getting through the day was her biggest challenge; she never had time to think about the rest of her life. She laughed again.

"Why do you keep laughing?" Shawn asked her.

Violet could tell he was trying to read her face but couldn't. He shrank back from her as if he was afraid of what she was going to say.

"There's a lot you don't know about me," Violet said. She could feel her ears turn red, and her heart beat faster.

"We can get to know each other as we take care of each other for the rest of our lives," Shawn said.

"I have a past, well, umm, a present," Violet said, stumbling over her words. "I've, I've been with...men before. I didn't wait for marriage."

Violet's words stung Shawn. *She didn't wait for marriage.* He leaned back and swallowed. This was not what he wanted to hear. Given that hugs were a challenge for him, he wasn't sure how he'd do in the lovemaking department. He wondered if he could measure up to the people Violet had been with before him and that filled him with dread.

He also wanted to be with someone who loved Shawn enough to save herself for him. That was important. He knew his grandparents waited until marriage and they never had issues in their bedroom; his grandpa confided that to Shawn while they were having an awkward conversation about sex while riding the E train.

Beads of sweat formed on Shawn's forehead. He could feel his breath quicken as he tried to figure out what to say to Violet. Her shoulders slumped and he could tell she was filled with regret. His mind wandered to moments in his past he regretted. There were countless times when he treated someone rudely or coldly and didn't realize it until later. Or moments when he was angry and lashed out, especially when he felt pushed into a corner. He lost count of the times when he was too stubborn to apologize.

For years, Shawn refused to say he was sorry to anyone he hurt because that's who he was, and people needed to accept that. His grandpa explained to Shawn how he couldn't be that way if he wanted people to like him and invited him to start going to church with them.

At church, Shawn learned about how Jesus treated others with kindness and compassion, even the people who killed him. And he claimed to be God! Shawn told his grandpa that he didn't understand why Jesus needed to die on a cross to forgive him, though.

"Forgiveness always has a cost," his grandpa said. "If I loaned you my car and you wrecked it, I'd forgive you, but someone would have to pay the cost to restore the car."

Shawn shrugged. "I don't want a car from God."

His grandpa laughed. "God gives us our lives, and each of our lives is like that car. We've all wrecked them to different degrees. But God is perfect. So, from God's point of view, we've all totaled our life cars."

Shawn felt a thickness in his throat at the idea that he had totaled his life.

His grandpa gave him a reassuring smile. "God wants to forgive us for turning away from him. But instead of us having to pay to be restored, God paid for it himself, on the cross. Jesus paid for our lives with his own life and then became alive again to show he was God and prove that everything he said was true."

It all sounded fantastical to Shawn, but when he studied more of the Bible, he felt overwhelmed by the lengths God went through to love and restore him. He liked how the Bible said Shawn could become a child of God if he put his faith in what Jesus did for him. He wanted in on that family.

One of Shawn's favorite Bible verses was when Jesus said, "There's no greater love than to lay down your life for your friends." When Shawn gave his own life over to God, he asked Jesus to forgive him for the choices he had made that he knew weren't right. He asked God for a new beginning and a new way to treat people.

As Shawn stood in front of the church building next to Violet, he wondered if this was now his chance to be the way he always prayed he could be. He could love Violet, no matter what. And besides, Violet said she was a follower of Jesus. So, they were part of the same spiritual family.

He looked up to her, hopeful. "Everyone has a past, but God gives us a new beginning. That's what that Amazing Grace song is all about."

Violet felt a heaviness in her stomach. She didn't expect that response from Shawn. She shifted her weight, unsure of what to say. A flush of adrenaline tingled through her body.

"I've read up on autism, but there's a lot I don't know," Violet said.

She had searched online and found a dating site for people on the spectrum, where people wrote about dates that went wrong, ways they could communicate better, and what not to do. She read about people struggling with how to process what came into their brains and how it could often be overwhelming.

Shawn let out a huge breath. "I need help making some decisions, paying bills, reading people's faces, maybe how to dress now and then, but Colin's been a big help there."

"And your family. I don't think they'd be too happy about this idea."

"If we're married, they'll have to accept you," Shawn said with certainty.

"Your grandma would think I'm after her money."

"I don't care." Shawn pulled the bow tie out of his pocket and quickly wrapped it around his neck. "Violet, I've been waiting my whole life for that special someone."

Violet was taken aback at seeing the bow tie. "You've been carrying that around?"

Shawn took a breath. "For when someone's colors sound right to me."

A yellow taxi pulled up next to them and honked. Shawn took something else from his pocket and held it out to her. The engagement ring.

Violet couldn't believe what was happening. Her heart thumped against her chest as if it was about to break through.

Shawn knelt, looked up at her, and smiled. "Will you marry me, Violet?"

She looked over the ring, her mouth wide open. It was a simple ring. Gold with intricate vines intertwined, bearing a sparkling diamond.

Years ago, Violet gave up the idea of this moment ever happening in her life. She thought she might get hitched someday if one of her clients wanted her badly enough to pay for her full time, or maybe she would earn extra cash by marrying someone to help them get a green card. But Violet didn't think she would marry someone who would know about her and still desire to be with her. Then again, Shawn didn't know everything about her. If he did, he wouldn't want anything to do with her. She couldn't handle that breakup. Not now.

Violet looked at the taxi and back to Shawn. And that ring. "Marriage didn't work out so well for my parents," she said.

"We can be different," Shawn said, holding his breath.

"Everyone thinks they'll be different. Maybe we should move in together first." She knew it was a bad idea and his grandmother would never go for it, but she couldn't figure out how to stop this conversation.

Shawn shook his head. "Not until I commit my life to you."

She looked between the taxi and Shawn. If he knew who she really was, he wouldn't be on his knee, he'd be pushing her away. "To you, marriage is a big deal. You shouldn't waste it on someone like me."

He gazed into her eyes. "Loving someone is never a waste."

Everything seemed to slow down for her. Here was the most loving man she had ever known, and he was asking her to marry him. There were parts of him that were different, and she didn't understand why, but the same was true of her. Except he didn't know what most of those parts were. He could never know.

She stood there for a moment, peering into his eyes. He held her gaze much longer than he usually did. But it started to feel like he was looking past her eyes, into her dark places where no one could look. She couldn't take it anymore. She turned, jumped into the taxi, and slammed the door. It quickly drove away.

Shawn's mouth dropped open as he watched her go. He looked stunned and crushed as he wiped tears from his eyes.

Inside the taxi, Violet sank into the back seat as they pulled into heavy traffic.

"Where do you wanna go?" the driver asked.

"I don't know," she said. The car slowed to a stop behind a garbage truck not far from Shawn while the driver waited for an answer. Horns honked. People yelled. It reminded Violet of the noisy chaos of her apartment building. And her life. Her forehead wrinkled, and her hands trembled as she processed this crush of emotions. She searched through her purse for one of her pills. They weren't there. When was the last time that slipped her mind? She debated what was right and wrong inside her head, and it led her to a dark corner of doubt.

She took out her compact to fix her tear-streaked makeup. There he was in the reflection of her mirror. He rose from the ground and stared after her, wiping his cheeks with his hands. *Do I want Shawn as my husband? Can I make that commitment? I can't even commit to a toothpaste flavor.*

She imagined a future without Shawn, and it dampened the new feeling of hope she had discovered after they started seeing each other. She closed the compact with a snap of finality.

Shawn clutched his stomach and slowly trudged back toward the entrance of the church. His body felt like it was crumbling in on itself. He gazed at the gray color of the sidewalk. The smoky tone pulsated to life. It hummed and grew louder and louder until—

A woman's hand tapped Shawn on his shoulder. He turned. Violet stood there, a half-smile on her face. She gave him a hungry embrace. Shawn instinctively pulled back and looked at her. "I'm sorry, I have to get used to that," he said.

"Of course."

Shawn slowly stretched his arms around her and pulled her in, accepting her embrace. The noise of the city turned quiet as they peered into each other's eyes. Shawn felt safe in Violet's arms.

After a long, life-altering pause, Violet nodded. "Let's do this."

Shawn beamed.

Violet's phone buzzed, and her whole body froze. She checked the screen. *Natasha got this one. Slow day. Check in.* She texted back. *Sorry, available whenever.*

"My audition got canceled," Violet said.

Shawn pressed his hand against his heart. "I couldn't be happier." He texted Ruth to tell her not to wait for him after church.

They headed across 83rd Street to Central Park. They strolled past the lake and headed across the Sheep Meadow, where New Yorkers threw Frisbees or enjoyed picnics on the grass. Shawn wanted to tell her about the history of the Sheep Meadow, how a shepherd used to stop traffic on the west drive so he could move the flock in and out of the park. But instead, they walked in silence as the magnitude of what just happened was still sinking in.

They headed across the park until Shawn heard the bark of a seal and realized they were at the entrance of the Central Park Zoo.

"I've never been here," Violet said.

"That means you haven't seen the Macaroni penguins," Shawn said. "And they have nothing to do with the noodles."

Violet laughed as he paid for their admission. He showed her the penguins. Then they ventured over to the snow leopards, where Shawn explained how he could relate to these animals the most. "They're completely out of place in New York City, and they struggle to communicate. That's basically me."

"I feel that way sometimes too," Violet said. Then her phone buzzed, and their time together was over.

Shawn slipped back into his grandma's apartment long after Ruth had fallen asleep that night. He rested his head on his pillow while staring at the bride and groom bobbleheads on his desk. Soon that would be him and Violet, and he felt breathless with excitement.

# CHAPTER 15

## LET HER GO

Violet plucked money out of Theo the bear and tucked it inside her purse. She planned to give the cash to Anton at the end of the night, to convince him she had her own clients while she was actually off getting married.

She stopped by a thrift store three blocks from her place and scoured the racks of clothes until she found a lace wedding dress, yellowed but not too badly. It didn't feel right for her to wear something pure white. If she happened upon a red wedding dress, she'd probably have to wear that. Shawn asked her to try to look like the women in the bridal websites, but that was the closest she could get. She did look like a bride from a wedding magazine, but one from twenty years ago.

At work, Shawn tested his algorithms and tried out his rating system on the remaining employees, all the while feeling like he was floating through the day. He took off from work early and rode the subway down to the Office of the City Clerk on Worth Street, where he would be meeting Violet. His heart raced while he waited.

Violet walked up the steps toward the Office of the City Clerk and felt like she was on her way to a costume party, not her own marriage. When Shawn caught sight of her, his eyes welled up. He was dressed in a tan suit with his black cummerbund and bow tie; they weren't tied correctly but were close.

"You look ravishing," he said. "Your dress sounds like hummingbirds."

She blushed. "You're not so bad yourself." Violet glanced around for Aleesha, who promised to be there as their witness.

"Over here," Aleesha said. She waved from the top of the steps, dressed in a tight, shimmering red dress. Shawn and Violet joined her.

"Haven't been to a wedding since I was a kid," Aleesha said. "It's exciting. Even though this one ain't real."

"It's real, Aleesha. What are you talking about?" Violet asked.

"I mean, it's not one of those big, fancy weddings."

"We're getting married, and that's what matters," Shawn said.

They stepped inside, filled out paperwork, took a number, and waited on the benches in the long sterile hallway.

Their number flashed on a screen above them. It was time.

The rotund City Clerk, a man in his forties with spiky black hair, held a look that was either no-nonsense or bored. It was hard to tell. He sat behind his desk in the dark, wood-paneled room and talked them through the ceremony while Aleesha chewed a wad of gum. They finally got to the moment when Shawn slipped the wedding band onto Violet's finger.

"I now pronounce you husband and wife," the City Clerk said. Then he picked something out of his teeth.

Shawn leaned forward and kissed Violet as if she was a delicate doll. When their lips touched, it felt like waves of electricity rippled through him, lighting him up with a delicious feeling. It started to overpower him, but he forced himself to bear it and pulled her in for another kiss. Then another, until the City Clerk muttered, "I've gotta keep this moving."

Shawn and Violet strode down the steps outside, beaming, while Aleesha checked her phone.

"I've gotta get going," Aleesha said. "Congrats, you two."

"Remember this is just between us," Violet said.

"I got you, girl," Aleesha said with a wink as she hurried toward the subway stop.

Everything around Shawn felt magnified. He reached out for Violet's hand. She smiled and gently clasped his. Ripples of energy coursed through him. He held on for a moment and let her go.

"I've been meeting with a therapist to learn how to desensitize myself."

"You don't have to do that for me," Violet said.

"I'm doing it for us," Shawn said.

Violet looked at the ring on her finger, then at her watch. "Unzip me?"

He unzipped her dress, and she pulled it off, revealing a blouse and jeans underneath. She stuffed the dress into her large purse with shaking hands. "We have to make a quick stop."

"We can't be late for our dinner." Shawn said.

Violet nodded. "I promise you, we've got time. It'll be a quick audition."

They took the R train to 8th Street and walked over to 6th Avenue, arriving at a small brick building sandwiched between a jewelry store and a nail salon. Violet gave Shawn an electric kiss, took a swig of her mouthwash, and disappeared inside.

Shawn leaned against the building and eyed the traffic passing by. He noticed little girls in tutus exit the ballet school across the street and construction workers lining up for an Umami burger next door. His heart felt full. *I'm finally married.* He felt more like an adult but not as much as he thought he would. Something gnawed at him, and he didn't know what.

Violet bounced out of the building's entrance an hour later.

"How'd you do?" Shawn asked.

She ran her fingers through her hair and flipped it back. "He wants me back."

"Wow," Shawn said, beaming. "That's a first."

"He really liked me," Violet said with a smile.

"Of course, he did."

She tucked rolled-up pages under her arm. "I just have to get these lines down by Thursday."

"I'm sure you'll get the part." Shawn gave her a big kiss. She pulled him in for a hug.

Colin, dressed in a coat and tie, fidgeted next to Ruth, who wore an elegant eggplant-colored dress. They waited inside the curved glass and steel wall of Le Cirque restaurant that faced an impressive stone courtyard. A sleek hostess with flowing blonde hair and long legs motioned for them to follow her into the dining area.

She escorted them to a corner table where she expertly pulled back a chair for Ruth while they both sat down. Walls of polished wood surrounded their table. A soaring tower stood in the middle of the room, displaying various statues of monkeys underneath a domed ceiling covered with folds of cloth.

"Do you know why Shawn wanted to meet here?" Ruth asked. "We usually only come here for special occasions."

Colin shrugged. "I wish I knew. It seems a little fancy for him." He tapped his spoon against the table.

Ruth cleared her throat. "We could have easily met at my place. But maybe he thought some people forgot where I live."

Colin crossed his arms. "How many times can I apologize for not going to Grandpa's funeral?"

Ruth narrowed her eyes. "You went to the Comedy Cellar."

Colin sighed. "To honor him. You know Grandpa. He'd tell us he felt like a newborn baby. No hair, no teeth, and he just wet himself. He loved it when we laughed. He'd always ask if we'd seen that grown-up Smurf movie. We'd ask him the name of it, and he'd say 'Avatar.'"

Ruth put the napkin in her lap. "I'm the one who needed you at the funeral. And I don't like it when people avoid me."

"I'm not avoiding you. I'm just busy with my life. Please stop treating me like I'm Dad."

Ruth clenched her napkin. Colin did remind her of her son since they had similar hair, eye color, and face shape. Still, she tried to not link them together.

"He's not avoiding me. He's avoiding being responsible for his sons," Ruth said.

Colin formed a steeple with his hands and pressed them to his lips. "Shawn and I will always be grateful you took us in. I hope you know that."

"Of course I do."

A waiter appeared and poured water into their glasses. Ruth took a sip. "Someone needed to look out for your future. Are you ready to look out for Shawn's? He was so close to falling in love with a disaster."

Colin nodded. "You know Grandpa would've taken me to that comedy club."

Ruth shook her head. She didn't want to get into this argument again, but they always seemed to end up on this path.

"When you pass away, I'll go to your favorite museum. That'll be my way of honoring you," Colin said. "The Whitney, right?"

"Depends on what they're showing. Otherwise, MOMA." She smiled a little. "Just promise you'll go after my funeral."

Colin placed his hand on his heart. "Promise."

Shawn stepped into the restaurant, holding Violet's hand, still in his tan suit but without his cummerbund or bow tie. Colin motioned to the door, and Ruth looked over. Her mouth opened in surprise.

Shawn saw Ruth and Colin at a table across the room. He couldn't tell what they were thinking, but he could see his grandma's mouth was hanging open. His heartbeat sped up as he led Violet over to them.

"Grandma, Colin, I'd like you to meet the newest member of our family."

Ruth and Colin both stood with confused looks on their faces, as if they were trying to figure out what he meant. Violet smiled uneasily and held out her hand for one of them to shake it. They didn't. Violet shrugged, pulled back a chair, and sat down. The rest of them silently followed.

Colin scratched his chin. "Uh...what do you mean?"

Shawn grinned. "We got married."

Violet held up her hand and flashed the rings. Ruth looked at them with an incredulous stare. "Tell me you're kidding."

"Now I'm saving up for a nice honeymoon," Shawn said.

Violet shook her head. "I told him I don't need that."

Colin jerked his head back. "Shawn, is this a joke?"

"You know I'm not good at pretend." He motioned to Ruth. "I thought Violet could stay at our place for now, until we get something on our own."

Ruth scowled. "It's not our place. It's mine. And absolutely not."

Shawn's smile faded. "But she's family now."

Ruth glared at Shawn. "She's a criminal."

Shawn winced. "Why would you say that?"

"I got the results of her background check and let me tell you, Olivia Black has a rich history. Ask her how many times she's been arrested."

Shawn turned to Violet. "You haven't been arrested."

Violet gazed down at the floor. Her shoulders slumped as if the room had closed in on her. "I told you I have a past."

Shawn's face turned red. "I can't believe this is how you're treating her. I finally found the one."

Colin gave Violet a flinty stare. "So did a lot of paying customers before you."

Shawn furrowed his eyebrows. "Paying customers?"

Violet took a breath. "Stop talking to him like he's a kid."

Ruth raised her voice an octave. "In some ways, he is a kid. After you give me back my rings, you can try explaining to him what it's like being arrested for solicitation," she said, holding out her hand.

"Solicitation?" Shawn's face creased with concern. His chest felt heavy. It became hard to breathe.

Violet glared back at Colin and Ruth. "He's a man with desires and passions and needs like everyone else."

A waiter in his fifties with a long, serious face and precise movements approached the table as Colin faced Violet. "Are you or are you not a prostitute?" The waiter quickly scurried away.

Violet shrank back from their judging eyes. She held her stomach, and her eyes grew moist. She peered into Shawn's confused face, then all around as if she was searching for something to say.

Suddenly, she pushed back her chair and stood up with a trembling chin. She rushed away from the table and out the door of the restaurant.

Shawn started to go after her, but Colin held him back. Shawn flailed and tried to push away from him.

"Let her go," Colin whispered.

"Violet!" Shawn yelled. The other diners turned to look at them. People scoffed. This was not the kind of restaurant where people yelled. Through the window, Shawn watched Violet rush away from the restaurant. The rolled-up pages dropped out of her purse as she ran off. "She's my bride," Shawn said, burying his face in his hands, not sure what that even meant anymore.

"She's a fraud," Ruth said. "Running all the way to the nearest pawn shop."

Shawn searched for words, tapping his fist against his lips. "She told me, she told me—" The shock had sucked the air out of his lungs.

"We know what she told you. I told you to be careful and you weren't. You were so obsessed with getting married," Colin said, shaking his head.

Shawn rocked back and forth and wrung his hands. A weight pushed the bottom of his stomach as if it was trying to pull him through the floor. The room felt like it was spinning. He slammed his fist against the table. People glanced over, whispering.

"We're sorry this happened, Shawn. We thought you left her," Ruth said gently.

Shawn let out a painful moan. A pudgy waiter approached with a concerned and irritated look, but Colin waved him away.

"Why would you do this without talking to us?" Ruth asked. "Marriage is serious business."

"She was going to take care of me. For the rest of my life," Shawn said, wiping tears from his eyes. The room seemed to dim.

"So that's why you married her. So, she could be your new grandma," Colin said.

Shawn shrugged. "I don't know how long Grandma will be around."

Ruth's nostrils flared. "That's no reason to go out and marry a whore."

"That wasn't all of it," Shawn said, scratching his cheek. "I felt something for her. Something real. I...I was with her at her auditions. She got a callback today."

Colin rolled his eyes. "She got called back to someone's bed."

Shawn looked between them, his face filled with uncertainty. "I don't believe you."

"Shawn, enough. Who do you trust? A lying prostitute or your family?" Ruth asked.

"Think about how many men she's been with, how many diseases she has," Colin said.

Ruth breathed rapidly and clutched her napkin. "I ...having a panic attack."

Shawn pushed up his sleeves. "Just keep telling her everything will be okay."

"Will it?" Ruth asked him with desperate eyes.

Shawn's look said he didn't know. Colin put his arms around Ruth as Shawn rushed away from their table, past confused waiters, and out the restaurant's front door. He raced across the courtyard and found the rolled-up pages Violet had dropped. He grabbed them and unrolled them. The sheets were blank.

Shawn felt suddenly paralyzed as a dark chill slid over him. He worked hard to breathe. Then he put one foot in front of the other and soon found himself moving forward. Shawn had to find Violet. He had to get answers. Pulling out his phone, he texted her over and over as he hurried to the subway but didn't get a response.

The train ride to Violet's side of town was noisy, hot, and crowded. Either the air conditioning was broken, or too many people were on the train. He transferred from the F train to the A train to the B83 bus.

Shawn stepped off the bus and paced down the sidewalk toward Violet's apartment, his hands in his pockets. The chilly night air licked the back of his throat while the colors around him shouted for his attention. A green neon "Hot Coffee" sign screeched, and a yellow streetlight buzzed. A pink deli sign gave off a metallic scream. Shawn squeezed his eyes shut; the noise was deafening.

Shawn dashed up the stairs to Violet's building and approached the entrance, stopping to catch his breath. He buzzed her apartment and waited. No answer. Buzzed again. Silence. He slid out his phone and texted her. *Where are you?*

No response.

Plopping down on the top of the stairs, he rubbed his stinging eyes and felt too heavy to move. His heart thudded dully against his chest.

He looked up to see Violet standing on the other side of the busy street, pacing back and forth with Anton at her side. Aleesha and Natasha stood nearby, waving and calling out to cars zipping by.

Shawn stood up and was about to yell Violet's name when a black limousine pulled up alongside her. Anton squeezed Violet tight to himself and leaned into the back of the limo. He seemed to be working out some kind of deal. Then, he opened the door for her.

"Violet!" Shawn screamed, running down the steps.

Violet met Shawn's eyes and froze. Startled. Her face showed a flash of regret and then hardened. Anton shoved her into the limousine. Shawn bolted across the street and turned to chase after the limo.

Anton grabbed his arm and pulled him back. "What the hell are you doing?"

"That's ...that's my wife," Shawn said, stammering.

Anton laughed and shook his head. "You got the wrong girl, pal."

The limousine turned the corner down the street, and Shawn realized he could never catch it. He hurried away from Anton, down the sidewalk toward the bus stop while fidgeting and squeezing his hands together. Aleesha and Natasha watched him go, glancing at each other with concern.

On the bus, he reached into his pocket and took out the picture of Amanda. The muscles clenched around his heart. It was happening all over again.

# CHAPTER 16

# DAMAGED GOODS

Shawn slumped over the edge of the stiff couch in Ruth's living room, his eyes stinging from tears, his heart shattered into pieces. His grandma perched next to him, crossing and uncrossing her legs. She reached out to rub his back, but he pulled away.

Colin carried over a glass of water in Shawn's favorite cup, the one with zeros and ones on it. He placed it on the table next to Shawn and took a seat on the chair. "Violet is damaged goods, bro. Return to sender,"

"We can get it annulled. No one needs to know it ever happened," Ruth said.

Shawn let out a long, slow sigh. "At least she was willing to take care of me."

Colin stood up, hunched over Shawn, and gave him a light tap on his cheek. "Come back to reality. That's not why you get married." Shawn winced from his touch; he felt like an exposed nerve. His face tensed with pain. Tears streamed down his cheeks.

Colin crossed his arms. "I barely touched you."

"You know he has heightened senses," Ruth said. "Remember in eighth grade when he got punched? He cried for a week."

That incident was forever stuck in Shawn's memory. He was taking the train home from Brooklyn on a Wednesday night and noticed a scrawny thirteen-year-old with bushy hair and yellow sneakers watching him read his book on superheroes. When Shawn arrived at his grandparent's stop, the yellow sneaker boy followed him and grabbed the book. Shawn held on and asked what he was doing. The boy tried to yank the book away while Shawn yelled that the book was a gift and belonged to him. The boy punched Shawn in his gut. Shawn doubled over and cried out so loud it frightened the boy. Sinking to the ground, Shawn had felt like he had been stabbed with a hundred knives.

Colin returned to the chair. "I'm sorry, bro."

Shawn nodded as Ruth handed him a tissue. He dabbed his tears and could feel his body start to relax.

"Ever thought of how you'd take care of her?" Colin asked.

"What do you mean?"

"Sounds like you made it all about you. That's not love, bro."

Shawn tried to find the right words to say, but they escaped him. He rubbed his forehead and looked at the colorless paintings on the walls, wishing Grandpa was there. Grandpa always had nuggets of wisdom at just the right moments or a funny joke if he didn't. One time, he told Shawn, "If you get married, don't let it become a three-ring circus." Shawn looked at him, confused. "You know, engagement ring, wedding ring, suffering," Grandpa said with a wink.

Shawn's insides quivered. He turned to Colin. "How do you know what love is? You can't even ask that girl out."

"At least I know what love isn't."

"Okay, enough," Ruth said. "We can take care of everything tomorrow. It's late."

"Yeah, I have to be at Think Coffee early," Colin said.

Ruth motioned to the couch. "You're welcome to stay here."

"Thanks, Grandma, but I should get back," Colin said.

"Good night," Shawn said, then then he trudged down the hall to his bedroom and shut his door. Leaning against his desk, he took a deep breath. His mind was still racing, processing the whirlwind of events. He peered up at the bride and groom bobbleheads on the shelf. Picking them up, he examined their fat, happy faces. Then he shoved them into his desk drawer and slammed it shut.

He stretched himself across his bed as his stomach spiraled downward, and his tears began to flow. An aching hole opened up inside of him, swallowing his hope. By the time he drifted off to sleep, he'd cried so much, it felt like he had no tears left.

That night, he dreamed he was on a boat constructed out of his grandmother's red velvet couch, floating in the ocean. Water quickly soaked through the cushions around him. He yelled to a nearby cruise ship for help. Then he noticed the boat was made from Popsicle sticks. It exploded with fire. The flames licking the ship were black and white.

The next morning, Shawn got ready for the day and raced out of the apartment before his grandma could say anything to him. He rushed past Douglas without saying good morning and avoided looking at anyone on the subway while he traveled down to the meatpacking district.

When the subway arrived at his stop, Shawn jumped off the train and hurried to the Exclusiv offices. No forced hellos from him that morning while he marched over to his workstation. Shawn sat down at his desk, his heart beating slow and sure. He ripped off the cheerful wedding pictures from his cubicle one by one. It stung to look at them now. They seemed too happy, too content, too fake. He crumpled them up and tossed them into his trashcan.

"I need an update on the rating system," Jake said, looming over him.

Shawn picked up a report from his desk and handed it to Jake. "It's ready to go. That's your score."

Jake scanned the piece of paper. There were a few summary sentences at the top of the page, and a large number two at the bottom. "I'm a two? Is that good?"

Shawn shrugged half-heartedly. "Ten is the best."

Jake raised an eyebrow. "Someone like me can't get a score that low."

Shawn took a long pause before responding. "It checks public records, analyzes how often you're mentioned online, number of friends—"

"You did it wrong," Jake said in a sharp tone.

"It's an objective rating of your past. Two out of ten," Shawn's voice raised slightly, as if Jake was bothering him. Jake glared at the workers around him. A few looked down at their desks. Flynn quickly busied himself at his computer.

Jake crumpled up the piece of paper. "This was a complete waste of time."

"I don't think so. People should know what they're getting into."

"No one will want a history score."

"Well, they should," Shawn said with a shaky voice.

Jakes's face tightened. "Unless you come up with something better, I can't keep shelling out money to have you here. I need something that makes our site stand out, not make people feel bad." He leaned in close to Shawn. "And don't ever run me through that program again."

Jake stormed back to his office, passing Tammy, whose shirt said, "Stop Wars" in the same font as "Star Wars."

"What happened to all your wedding pics?" Tammy asked Shawn as she approached his desk.

Shawn shook his head. "They were all pretending. Everyone is pretending."

Tammy eyed him over. "That doesn't sound like you."

"I thought I found someone," he said, giving a slow, disbelieving head shake. "Turns out she wasn't who I thought she was."

Tammy picked a piece of lint off her shirt. "Welcome to relationships. Everyone hides who they are until they know they'll be loved and accepted. Do you love her?"

Shawn buried his face in his hands. "I thought I did."

"Did you love her for who she is or who you want her to be?"

Shawn looked away from her, thinking.

"Love is friendship that has caught on fire. Might wanna figure out if you're burning," Tammy said.

"Burning?" Shawn asked.

"If you love her."

He looked at her blankly. "How?"

"Don't ask me. My love sensor broke years ago," Tammy said.

Shawn tilted his head to the side. "What's a love sensor?"

"Forget about it. Just remember the party tonight. We're short on RSVPs, so Jake needs everyone there. Make sure you look gangsta." Tammy gave him a wave and continued through the office.

Shawn nodded. He had forgotten about the party. He used to beg to go to them; now, he was dreading it. The rest of the day, Shawn felt like he was stuck in molasses. He left work early and stopped by Think Coffee.

Colin looked up when Shawn entered the café. "You're here earlier than normal. I'm surprised you're here at all."

"I need you to go to this party with me tonight," Shawn said, handing him the invitation. Colin looked it over and gave it back.

"I don't know." Colin looked past him, then darted his eyes away. Shawn glanced over and noticed Laura sitting a few tables away from the barista bar. She peered up at them.

Shawn whispered to Colin. "Let's make a bet. I think Laura will say 'yes' if you ask her out. She keeps looking at you."

"I don't know why she looks up here." Colin grabbed a towel and scrubbed the barista counter. "You didn't even have a best man."

"It was a quick ceremony."

"I always thought you cared about our family."

Shawn stepped closer to Colin. "I do."

Colin pulled away from him. "Then you should've told me what was going on."

"I thought she was the one." Shawn shook his head and swallowed hard. "You can help me get the annulment." He choked back tears. Squeezing his eyes shut for a moment, he collected himself. He wasn't used to riding a rollercoaster of emotions. "Do you want to go to this party with me or not?" He could feel a headache coming on.

Colin sighed. "I can't. I've got an interview tomorrow. Bright and early."

"Interview?"

"For a teaching job."

"Why didn't you tell me?"

"Because I hate doing things just because people tell me I should." Colin tossed his towel down on the counter. "I probably get that from Dad."

"If you hate it so much, you shouldn't tell me what I should do."

"I'm looking out for you. That's what brothers are for." Colin said. "Even though I haven't done a good job of that with you."

Shawn paused and looked up at Colin. "How do you know if someone is the one?"

"Well, you shouldn't love someone just because of what she can do for you," Colin said, matter-of-factly.

"But I miss being with her. Talking to her. Her smile. The way she walked. Every night I prayed God would make her mine. I thought he did."

"If she loved you, she wouldn't have gone back to sleeping around, right?"

Shawn nodded. He hadn't thought about that before, but Colin was right. Violet dedicated herself to Shawn for the rest of her life, and then right after they tied the knot, she was with another man. Then hours later, it happened all over again. That was supposed to be their special wedding night. And who knows how many men she's been with since then?

"I'll help you find someone who would never cheat on you. Someone you love so much you can't stand the idea of her being with someone else. She's out there." Shawn smiled half-heartedly.

Colin stepped out from behind the counter and pulled Shawn toward Laura's table. "Or maybe she's right here." Laura looked up from her coffee, and Shawn could feel his pulse quicken. He wasn't ready for this. Colin motioned to Shawn. "Free coffee for a week if you go to a party with my brother tonight."

"You don't have to do that," Shawn said to Colin.

"Come on, bro, you need a date." He turned to Laura. "It's for his work, they throw great parties. I promise you'll love it. Right, Shawn?" Shawn felt backed into a corner. All he could do was nod and smile.

Laura fingered her necklace. "I might be free tonight."

Colin smiled, and Shawn stared down at the floor. "Then it's a date," Colin said. "I'll even pay for your costume."

"Sounds fun," Laura said.

"Thanks," Shawn said to Colin. Before Violet came along, he would've jumped at the chance to go out with someone like Laura but now he was feeling numb and uncertain, adrift on a confusing sea of love.

Shawn handed Laura his phone. "Put your number in, and I'll text you the details."

She took his phone and typed in her number while Shawn exchanged glances with Colin. Laura handed the phone back to him.

"I should get going, then," Shawn said. "We can meet there."

"That sounds good," Laura said.

Colin walked Shawn over to the door of the café. "I think this could be really good for you."

"But you're the one interested in her," Shawn said.

Colin pulled the door open. "You can tell me if she's worth dating." Shawn nodded as he stepped out of Think Coffee, on his way to find a costume shop.

Dressed in a black and white pinstriped gangster suit with a black fedora, Shawn shifted his weight from one foot to the other outside the warehouse's entrance next to the glittering Manhattan Bridge. A group of gangsters and flappers stood in a velvet-roped line next to him, waiting to get inside the party.

Laura glided down the sidewalk toward Shawn, wearing a tight flapper dress covered in beads and sequins with shimmering fringe. A headband with a diamond broach and several pearl necklaces completed her look.

"It's fun getting dressed up," Laura said to Shawn.

He shrugged. "I get dressed up every day."

Shawn led her to the front of the velvet ropes, where a stocky bouncer let them inside.

A jazz band jammed from the stage at the back of the large, airy warehouse. Shawn navigated through the crowd while Laura tried to keep up.

"A lot more people here than I thought," Laura said.

Shawn nodded as he pulled a pair of earplugs out of his pocket and put them in. Laura twirled her necklace. "Your brother told me parties like this can be tough for you. I've got a nephew who's autistic."

Shawn hung his head. "So, this is a pity date."

"Not at all. I wanted the free coffee." Laura looked at him blankly and then broke out into a smile. "I'm kidding. People don't ask me out as much as you might think."

"It's because you're so beautiful it startles people."

"Oh. Thank you," Laura said, touching her throat. She glanced around. "I'm going to find the restroom. Do you want something to drink?"

"Not from the restroom."

She laughed. "I didn't mean..."

Shawn grinned. "I know."

"I, um. I'll be back." She made her way through the crowd.

Shawn glanced around for Tammy or Flynn or someone from the office, but he didn't recognize anyone. He chewed on one of his fingernails. He felt lost. Uncomfortable. Alone. The dazzling lights and trumpet sounds pressed in on him.

Jake took a seat at the bar, dressed in a flashy gold gangster suit with a plastic machine gun dangling from his neck. He held court with two women. Shawn straightened and realized these weren't just any women, they were Aleesha and Natasha, both dressed in short flapper skirts with long beaded necklaces circling their necks. *Is Violet nearby?* Shawn wrung his hands, not sure what to do.

Jake pointed Aleesha and Natasha toward two men in their twenties who leaned against the other side of the bar, both in oversized dark suits. The taller man had red hair, a goatee, and a belly. The other was thin with black curly hair and broad shoulders. The men were trying to strike up conversations with a couple of flappers, but the women only paused for a moment and then moved on.

Aleesha and Natasha nodded to Jake and made their way over to the men, turning on their smiles. When they approached, the men immediately brightened. Aleesha ran her fingers across one of their collars, while Natasha pressed in close to the other. The men grinned and soaked in the attention. Shawn cringed as he watched Aleesha and Natasha laugh and flirt with them. Their conversation looked so real, but Shawn knew it wasn't.

Aleesha whispered into her man's ear. He nodded and said something to the other guy, who smiled devilishly. Together, they walked toward the warehouse doors where people still streamed inside. Their night was obviously just beginning.

Shawn followed them, curious to see what would happen next. Before heading out the door, Aleesha stopped and gave Jake a kiss on his cheek.

"Where's Violet?" Jake asked.

"Busy," she said.

"Tell her I asked about her," Jake said with a wink. Then he smacked her butt.

Shawn's eyes grew wide. An invisible hand punched him in his chest. He felt ill and angry. *Was Violet with Jake? Was he her client?* He had to find Violet. Right now.

# CHAPTER 17

## A PRICE TAG ON HER

Shawn buzzed Violet's intercom over and over. Her voice finally crackled through the speaker. "Yeah?" she asked, annoyed.

"It's Shawn. Can I come up?"

A few moments passed before her voice sputtered through again. "You can do whatever you want." Shawn didn't know what she meant by that, but the door buzzed, he opened it and headed inside to the elevators. They smelled like cigarette smoke and took forever as they squeaked up floor by floor. *God, please help me. Please make something good out of all this.* The elevator dinged.

Shawn rushed down the hallway until he found her apartment. He planted his feet firmly, then knocked on the door. Violet cracked it open, pulling a blue bathrobe tightly around herself.

She eyed his gangster outfit. "Looks like I'm underdressed."

"It's a work party."

"Uh-huh. Didn't think I'd see you again."

Shawn wrung his hands and rocked on his heels. "I need to know why you were at the pimps and hos party."

Violet scoffed. "So you could break my heart. Obviously."

Shawn's voice strained. "You know my boss, Jake."

She leaned against the door frame. "Sure. We all do."

Shawn's face darkened. "What does that mean?"

Violet shrugged. "He likes to give his party guests encouragement. Me and the girls are very…encouraging."

Shawn clenched his jaw and felt like a vice was squeezing his heart. He forced himself to peer into her eyes and stepped closer. "I need to know what that means."

Violet swallowed. "He fixed it up with Anton for us to spend time with guys at the party. Jake thought we'd fit in with the girls from your app. He's not that bad. Gives us cab fare. Good tipper."

Shawn squeezed his hands together as he glared at her. "Have you *been* with him, Violet?" His lips trembled. He felt like his stomach was bottoming out.

Violet's face hardened. "Why should you care? We're over. No more using each other."

"I didn't use you."

"You needed someone to babysit you, and I needed a ticket out of here." Her words stung, then pierced through him. He fixed his gaze on her robe as his eyes filled with tears. The blue color moaned. Shawn covered his face with his hands. Violet reached back inside her apartment and handed him the rose plant. "Here. You take care of something for a change."

Shawn took the plant with quivering hands and noticed the leaves falling off the red blooms. "You should've told me what you do."

She put her hand on her hip. "So you'd treat me like your grandma does? No thank you."

"You lied to me about the auditions."

"Guess you can't trust everything you hear."

"You said you got a callback."

Violet crossed her arms. "So, I'm not who you thought I was. Time to move on. This is obviously where I belong."

Shawn wished with all his might that he could read her expressions. Her words wounded him, but he didn't know if he should believe them. Shawn silently prayed for God to help him. Then he peered into her green eyes. "I miss laughing with you, talking about the day, having a meal—"

"You'll get over me," Violet said.

She slammed the door in his face.

Shawn jolted backward in shock. His insides froze, and it felt like his heart came to a stop. He wasn't sure what to do. Here was a woman he connected with, shared his life with, and actually married. And she just slammed the door shut on their future. Shawn felt like he was being dragged underwater, and he didn't know how much longer he could hold his breath.

He wished he had run his algorithms on Violet. If he knew how low her score was, he wouldn't have wasted his time dating her, laughing with her, finding out about her life…

He started down the hallway but stopped. Questions filled his mind. *If God doesn't hold my past against me, how can I hold Violet's against her? Is it about the past or the future?* He squeezed his eyes shut and thought everything through. Slowly pivoting around, he returned to Violet's door and spoke softly. "Do you miss me?"

"I don't miss any of my clients," she said from the other side of the door.

He scrunched up his face. "I wasn't a client."

"A non-paying client. The worst kind."

Her words were barbed wire against his skin. He couldn't take it any longer. All he could do was let out a scream. "Aaaaahhhhh!"

Violet swung her door open. "You wanna get me in trouble?"

Shawn's eyes widened. "I thought you cared about me. I thought we had a future."

"That's all part of what I do. Maybe you'd have seen that if you weren't so autistic."

Her words felt like a knife plunging into Shawn's heart. His eyes welled up with tears, and his whole body trembled. He noticed her face alter and she blinked a lot. *What does that mean?*

"Your face changed," Shawn said.

Her expression tensed. "Please leave."

"I got so mad when I thought you'd been with Jake," Shawn said, choking out his words.

She held onto the doorframe. "You shouldn't care."

"He doesn't deserve you. I don't deserve you either." He exhaled and peered at her. "You're not a replacement for my grandma." He looked her deep in her eyes, enduring the electric intensity. "I love you, Violet."

Her face became stony. "You're not the first guy to say that."

Shawn wiped tears from his eyes and nodded. He realized his relationship with Violet was over. As he turned away, he noticed something peeking out from the bottom of Violet's blue robe. The train of her wedding dress.

He reached over and pulled her robe open to see more of her dress. He slowly slipped the robe off her shoulders, letting it crumple onto the floor. She stood there, in her yellowed wedding gown, with a pained smile on her face. "When's a girl like me going to get a chance to wear a dress like this again?"

Shawn noticed Violet was wearing her wedding rings. He motioned to them. "Did you wear those when you were with your clients?" Her mouth opened as if she was going to say something. Instead, she turned and disappeared into her apartment. Shawn stood there waiting, not sure what to do. She didn't return, so he followed her inside.

Her apartment still bore the fingerprints of Shawn's organizing. Barney wagged his tail from behind his fence in the kitchen. Violet paced around the apartment. "You shouldn't have run after me the other night. You shouldn't be here now."

"I'm here because I love you."

Violet scoffed. "You can't love me after everything I've done."

"That's why I'm standing here. Let me love you."

Violet shook her head. "It's not right. You were my failed escape plan. My future inheritance. That's all."

Shawn pointed to the corners of her apartment where he could see paper wedding bells and a sign that read *Just Married*. "I don't think that's all."

Violet let out a huge breath. "I thought we could have a special first night."

"But then you lied about that audition."

"I thought if I kept that up, I could hide what we were doing from my pimp and buy us some time. I just went through the motions with that guy. But after the restaurant, when I saw you run after me...I couldn't be with anyone else."

"But I saw you get in that car."

"Anton forced me in. But I pretended I was sick, and nothing happened. I've been here ever since figuring out what to do."

"You weren't going to let me in."

"Because you're too good to be true." She stood across from him, leaning against the door to the bathroom, her lips trembling. "I always thought it would be hard to love someone. To really love someone. But I never realized how hard it would be to let someone love me."

She took a moment. "I kept telling myself over and over, you were my failed escape plan. Nothing else. But I've missed the way you see the world, your bad jokes, the way you care about me."

A strange sense of relief washed over Shawn. Violet opened the refrigerator door and pulled out a small two-tier white wedding cake. On top of the cake were two bulldogs dressed as a bride and groom. "They ran out of people."

She grabbed two forks and carried the cake over to the kitchen table. She pointed to an ant farm on the kitchen counter, still in the box. "In case you wanted to raise ants together." Violet took a bite of the cake. "I thought we'd come back here and then make plans to run away. Don't know why I thought my pimp would ever let me go."

Shawn sat down on the chair across from her and pulled close to the table. "When were you going to tell me about your past?"

"As soon as I knew you really loved me."

"But I couldn't really love you if I didn't know about your past."

"Guess I know that now." She stuffed another piece of cake into her mouth.

Shawn hesitated, not sure what to do.

Violet pointed to the cake. "It's gluten and dairy-free."

Shawn brightened. He grabbed the other fork and cut off a piece. Shawn held it out to feed her as if they were at their wedding. He moved it around, just missing her mouth. She giggled. He finally made it in. She pulled off a clump of cake with her hand. Shawn smiled. She aimed it toward his mouth and smeared some on his nose.

Shawn pulled out his phone. "This is a song I always wanted to play for our first dance." He scrolled through his phone. "It's called 'A Kiss To Build A Dream On.'" He placed his phone on the table and turned the volume up. The slow, jazzy, Louis Armstrong song filled the room. Shawn stood up and offered his hand to her. "I've been practicing desensitization techniques."

Violet smiled. "You know just what to say." She took his hand. They held each other close and swayed to the music. Their first dance. Shawn felt her warm body against his. His pulse quickened, and the room started to cave, but he kept his breathing slow and steady to keep it all under control.

Barney gazed at them from the kitchen and drifted off to sleep.

The song faded away, and Shawn and Violet both yawned. Shawn checked his watch. It was late.

Violet reclined across her bed in her wedding dress and beckoned him over.

Shawn could feel his heart thud against his chest as he followed her to the bed. He stood at the foot, unsure of what to do.

"You'll have to take off your shoes," Violet said.

He nodded and quickly kicked them off. Climbing onto the bed next to Violet, he felt like he was on fire. He sank into the pillow next to her and gazed into Violet's eyes. She caressed his cheek. His whole body tingled with waves of excitement. What was off-limits to him his whole life was now an open door. This was his wife across from him. His actual wife.

He closed his eyes to thank God for this moment. The algorithms he had been working so hard on paraded through his mind. He could see what was wrong with them. Why did he only concentrate on everything from the past? He started thinking about the origins of the word *algorithm*. Wasn't it named after the Latin translation of a book written by a Persian mathematician who was also an astronomer and geographer? What was his name? That's right, al-Khwarizmi. How long ago was that? The 800s?

Violet studied Shawn's face, not sure why he closed his eyes or what would happen next. Her body felt stiff. Even though she knew they were married, she didn't feel ready for what married couples do on their wedding night. She wondered how sex could ever feel like love for her. Maybe if they had a more official kind of wedding, something that didn't feel rushed? Would that make it feel more real to her?

She combed her hand through his hair. "Your techniques really work."

Shawn didn't respond. Violet gave him a nudge. Shawn's breathing became steady, and Violet realized he had drifted off to sleep. She relaxed and scooted closer to him, pressing her head against his chest, which rose and fell with each breath. It felt comforting. Peaceful. This was not the way she imagined her day would end. Whenever she was with a man, she was counting down the minutes until it was over and hoping it would end without her getting hurt. But here was a man she wanted to stay with. Someone who actually loved her. Knowing that made her feel safe and content.

The sun was up now, washing the apartment with a golden hue. Violet and Shawn dozed in her bed, he in his pinstriped suit and she in her wedding dress from yesteryear, entwined in each other's arms. Violet's phone lit up and buzzed on the nightstand next to her. She managed to turn it off without looking at it. Then she wrapped her arms around Shawn and fell back asleep.

The bang, bang, bang on Violet's door woke them up with a start.

Anton yelled from the other side. "Sweetie, I know you're in there."

Violet looked at Shawn with fear, unsure of what to do.

"Can't afford you being sick anymore. Neither can you," Anton said. "I'm breaking this door down in three, two…"

Violet slid off the bed. Shawn grabbed her arm, but she pulled away. "Coming!" Violet shouted as she hurried to the door. She opened it just enough to see Anton, who loomed in the doorway, hanging off the top of the doorframe.

"You've got a star client waiting," Anton said with a wink. "The big tipper." He looked over her dress. "What's with the getup?" Anton pushed the door open all the way and spotted Shawn.

"I'm with…a friend," Violet said.

Shawn stepped off the bed, "Her husband." Violet glanced at Shawn with a slight smile, as if she was happy to hear him say that.

Anton looked between them with a glare on his face. "You can play house when she's off the clock."

Shawn put his arm around Violet and could feel her body tense up. His heartbeat quickened as beads of sweat formed across his neckline. Anton snarled at Shawn, then ripped Violet away from him, shoving her into the hallway. Barney barked.

"Shut the hell up!" Anton yelled to the dog. He pointed a finger to Shawn. "And you. Don't test me."

Shawn stood his ground. "She doesn't work for you anymore."

Anton looked at Shawn and scoffed. "She's mine until she pays off her debt."

"She doesn't have any debt to you," Shawn said, rubbing the back of his neck.

Violet looked down to the floor, her hair falling across her face.

"New York is pricey, and this place ain't cheap," Anton said.

"How much?" Shawn asked Anton.

A grin spread across Anton's face. "Too much."

Shawn took a quick breath. "How much to release her from you?"

Anton pushed his shoulders forward. "She ain't for sale."

"You put a price tag on her every night," he took a step forward. "Five thousand?""

Anton sized up Shawn. It looked like his wheels were turning. "Ten."

Shawn didn't know where he would get ten thousand dollars. "Then you'll let her go?"

Anton moved in close to Shawn so only he could hear. "You real about this?"

Shawn nodded.

Anton whispered. "Then this is between you and me. Anyone else gets involved, and you don't see your 'wife' again, or your Central Park West grandma. Got it?"

Shawn's body froze with fear. *How does he know where we live?* He nodded. "And you'll keep her from being with anyone else."

Anton made steeple fingers with his hands. "For fifteen thousand, I'll keep this little money-maker off the streets and under my watchful eye."

Shawn nodded. "Okay."

"See you real soon," Anton said with a smirk. Then he pointed Shawn out the door.

As he passed by Violet, she whispered to him, "I love you too." Shawn's heart fluttered.

# CHAPTER 18

## YOU HAVE TO LEAVE NOW

"Grandma?" Shawn yelled as he dashed into Ruth's apartment. No answer. He looked through all the rooms. A new canvas leaned on her easel in her bedroom, but there was no sign of grandma. He looked at his phone and noticed he had several missed calls from her. He rang her cell, but she didn't answer, so he left a voicemail.

Shawn paced around the living room, thinking about how intimidating Anton looked, all the money he needed to find, Violet trapped in her apartment. He sensed a dark feeling creeping over him as if something terrible were lurking around the corner of his life up ahead. He prayed for God to help him, to work everything out.

He stopped pacing and retreated into his bedroom. Sitting on the edge of his bed, he took out the picture of Amanda from his pocket. It had become yellowed and wrinkled. She wouldn't want me hanging onto the past like this. She'd want me to figure out my future.

Shawn gently kissed the picture and placed it inside the top of his desk. He needed to keep moving forward, not looking back. He heard the front door open.

Shawn rushed into the living room. Ruth stepped inside, dressed in a trench coat and a flowery dress.

"Where have you been?" Shawn asked.

"The cemetery. What about you? I was worried. You never answered your phone."

"Oh no. Grandpa's anniversary. Did you go alone?"

"I went with Colin and...a friend," she said mysteriously. It was the first time she took Douglas to Greg's tombstone. She usually embarked on those weekly trips by herself, but Ruth thought it was finally time to include the man who was thawing her heart. She was surprised when Colin showed up to accompany her, and Colin was equally surprised when Douglas opened the front door and kept following them through it.

Ruth told Grandpa about Douglas and some of their dates when they reached the gravestone while Colin listened with wide eyes. By the end of her conversation, Colin was cheering for them. Ruth didn't think it was appropriate for Colin to assert his own opinion to Grandpa, but she secretly appreciated it.

"Ready for the annulment?" Ruth asked Shawn.

Shawn swallowed. "We're going to stay together."

Ruth crossed her arms. "What?"

"I just need to buy her back."

"Buy her back?" Ruth asked, raising an eyebrow.

"From her pimp. To pay off her debt. Fifteen thousand dollars."

Ruth laughed. "You don't need to buy an impossible marriage for fifteen thousand. You can get that for free."

Shawn wrung his hands. "Grandma, I know you have that kind of money. I can do five thousand, but that's getting cash advances and giving everything I've got."

Ruth whisked the dishwasher open and started emptying it. "Maybe he'll give you a discount. Does he take coupons?"

"Grandma—"

Ruth grabbed the glasses from the dishwasher and banged them down inside the cabinet. "I've spent my whole life taking care of you. And when it mattered most, you married in secret. Without bagpipes."

"Bagpipes?"

"You told your grandpa you'd have bagpipes at your wedding. To honor our heritage." Ruth stacked the plates in the cabinet.

Shawn shuffled his feet. "I thought she was the one."

"A prostitute? God help you." She slammed the dishwasher shut, picked up a cloth from next to the sink, and began furiously dusting the apartment.

"You wanted me to marry someone who was like a woman from the Bible," Shawn said.

"Because you'd be a lot better off."

"Rahab is a woman from the Bible. She was a prostitute. God turned her life around. And she was related to Jesus." Ruth shook her head in disbelief as she dusted the lamp next to the couch. "And what about Mary Magdalene? She had her issues. Then she was the first one to see Jesus rise from the dead."

"Please," Ruth said with a sigh.

"If God can help someone who isn't perfect, which is all of us, why can't you?" He stood up a little straighter. "I think it's because you don't want to love anymore."

"Now you're being mean." She returned to the kitchen and grabbed a box of bird feed from the cupboard above the sink. Shawn followed her over to Cloudy and Sunny, who were chirping. "I have never been in love. It is not my way or my nature, and I do not think I ever shall. Jane Austen said that. I looked it up."

"I was joking when I said I wanted to live like one of her novels."

Shawn's face flushed red. "Well, the joke's on our doorman. And my wife. And your colorless paintings. I hope those aren't your only purpose in life."

Ruth dropped birdseed into the feeding trough. "You're late for work. And you better get my rings back. Otherwise, that will be my new life purpose." She stormed down the hall and disappeared inside her bedroom, slamming her door.

On the subway, Shawn's thoughts were consumed with raising enough money to release Violet. He couldn't get a bank loan that quickly, especially without any collateral. He also had a nagging feeling that his job was on the line after his last conversation with Jake. He arrived at Exclusiv and swiped his key card across the pad next to the door several times, but the light stayed red.

Finally, the door swung open as a couple employees made their way into the hallway. Shawn slipped past them into the offices. When he arrived at his desk, he discovered his belongings were packed up in a box.

Shawn motioned to Flynn, who pulled off his headphones. "Someone moved my stuff."

Flynn's eyes darted around the room. "Oh, um, I heard they left messages for you."

"About what?" Shawn asked.

Flynn stood up and gritted his teeth. "I don't think you work here anymore."

Shawn's stomach clenched. If he had no income, there was no chance he could rescue Violet. He nodded to Flynn and marched past him to Jake's office, with a determined look. He knocked on Jake's door while saying a silent prayer.

"Enter," Jake said from inside. Shawn stepped into his office where a mounted deer head hung above the desk. Pictures of sexy women wearing intelligent looking glasses dotted the walls. A bottle of gin served as a paperweight. Jake looked up from his desk and wrinkled his brow. "I hope you have more luck finding your next job than you've had finding your next date."

"I know you've been spending money to help me come up with something to set us apart. What if we don't make it about the past but about the future? We can ask people where they see themselves going, who they'd like to be with, what they'd like their future to be all about. Create algorithms based on their answers," Shawn said.

"I don't think so," Jake said.

"I can run you some examples. No one else has something like this."

Jake leaned back on his chair and propped his feet on the desk. "It can't be too perfect. I want people looking, not finding. Finding is bad for business."

"This will keep them looking for someone who matches their score. We can call it a 'future score.' It'll be unique to our app."

"I like uniqueness." Jake gazed off as if he were thinking it all through. "What kind of future score do you think I'd have?"

Shawn looked down to the ground. He knew this was a moment when he should be careful about what he said. Violet's future could depend upon it. "I think you might have a pretty good future score."

Jake nodded. "You've got one more chance."

"Thank you," Shawn said. Then he took a moment. "I, um, also need something else."

"I don't have all day," Jake said.

"I need your help with Violet. To get her out of prostitution." Shawn said, a little too loudly. A few employees glance their way.

Jake pressed his lips together and lowered his voice. "I hired a few performers. What they do on their time is up to them."

Shawn could feel his heartbeat accelerate. A weight pushed down on his shoulders. Shawn knew he needed to tread carefully, but he also knew he wasn't very good at that. "I'm not going to tell the police unless you do it again. But I need you to loan me ten thousand against my future salary so I can buy Violet's freedom."

Jake looked him over. His face tensed, and then he burst out laughing. "You're hilarious."

"I'm being very serious."

Jake closed his eyes and rubbed the middle of his forehead. "That sounds more like a threat than a request."

"And you've got a growing business. Maybe you can find a place for the women here," Shawn said, taking a step closer.

"You already took me for a hundred," Jake said, his face hardening. He pulled some hundred dollar bills out of his wallet. "Here are a few more. For the cause. I just hired entertainers. Nothing more. Now go get to work on that future score if you want a future."

Shawn stood there, not sure what to do. It felt like his feet had been nailed to the floor. Jake glared at him. Shawn forced himself to glare back. Jake threw up his hands. "Fine." He opened his wallet and pulled out a few more bills. "That makes a thousand. Best I can do. But I never want to hear about this entertainer nonsense again."

Shawn swept up the bills and nodded to Jake. Then he turned and let himself out of the office, stuffing the hundreds into his pocket. It wasn't enough, but at least it was a move in the right direction.

Shawn returned to his desk, with his arms hanging limply at his sides, a hopeless look on his face. Tammy stopped by wearing a T-shirt that featured a recycling symbol. "No more parties for me," Shawn said, waving her away.

Tammy put her hands on her hips. "I overheard you talking to Jake. I'm proud of you for standing up to him. He's a work in progress, but he's coming along."

Shawn logged into his computer with his back to her. "You don't know what he's been doing."

"Don't be so sure," Tammy said, smiling weakly. She could feel her face suddenly become hot. Shawn looked at her with a curious look. Tammy glanced around and stepped closer to Shawn. "The thing is …that's how I first got hired."

Shawn raised one of his eyebrows. "As an entertainer?"

Tammy nodded. "Then Jake got me a job here. Took me off the streets."

Shawn looked at her with widened eyes. Tammy expected him to recoil or make a cruel joke. He hadn't done that before; she just didn't know how her coworkers would respond when they knew the truth. She felt relief that his look didn't change.

"Thanks for telling me," Shawn said. "I wish he'd help all the women."

Tammy felt a rush of encouragement. She smiled. "That's throwing him into the deep end to teach him how to swim."

Shawn's look turned to confusion. "Never mind," Tammy headed toward Jake's office. "I'll see what I can do. Violet has always been nice to me. Just make sure her ring doesn't have one of those blood diamonds."

Shawn watched Tammy go into Jake's office, and he waited. And waited. He texted Colin and asked him for a loan. Colin asked him why. Shawn texted him about Violet's situation. Colin texted back a sad face emoji but said he couldn't help. Shawn asked him why he couldn't but didn't hear anything back.

Tammy emerged from Jake's office, shaking her head. She approached Shawn's desk. "Looks like that's all he's going to do for now," Tammy said. "But here." She pulled a few twenties from her pocket. "It's not much, but maybe it'll help a little."

"Thanks, Tammy"

She nodded as she continued across the office. Shawn turned toward his desk and gazed off into the distance. He was closer but still needed thousands of dollars.

At lunchtime, Shawn left work and headed over to Think Coffee to try to convince Colin in person. When Shawn stepped into the café, Colin worked the espresso machine and didn't look happy to see him. "I gave you a shot with Laura. She said she couldn't find you, and you never texted her back."

"I want to be with Violet. I know she'll need counseling and help to—"

"That wasn't right, Shawn," Colin handed a cappuccino to an NYU student.

Shawn nodded. "You're right. I'll tell her I'm sorry."

"I'm giving her free drinks to make up for it. Not so cheap. Especially that Gegarang coffee you like so much."

Shawn shuffled his feet and wrung his hands. "Maybe I can help pay for that."

"And you got me in trouble this morning. My manager saw me texting when I should've been helping a customer. She asked me why, and I told her about your crazy plan."

"It's not crazy," Shawn said.

Colin tilted his head to the side. "My manager didn't think so either. She told me they named our Gegarang coffee after the village in Indonesia where we buy the coffee from. She said our partnership helps them escape being slaves. That's why we buy so much of it. Also, it's earthy, spicy, clean and sweet with a syrupy body—"

"Why are you telling me this?"

"When she told me that, it made me realize I could help rescue someone who's enslaved." Colin pulled an envelope out of his pocket. "It's two thousand. All I could do."

A smile broke out across Shawn's face. He took the envelope and pulled Colin in for a hug. Colin's eyes welled up.

"Why do your eyes look like that?" Shawn asked.

Colin laughed. "You never hug me, bro." Shawn nodded, unsure what to say. Colin pointed to the envelope. "That was worth it."

As the clouds drank in the rest of the evening light and the sky turned blue-black, Shawn's hopes for collecting the rest of Violet's ransom equally dimmed. He took a taxi all the way out to her apartment, wondering if Anton would accept the amount he raised. *Please, God, help us,* he prayed.

Shawn punched in the code to let himself into Violet's building and took the elevator up to her floor. He hurried down the hallway and was surprised to find her door open and the lights off. Shawn pushed the door open, stepped inside, and looked around, but it was hard to see in the dark.

He switched on the overhead light. "Violet?" She was curled up in bed, buried under a pile of covers, face down.

"The lights. Too bright," Violet said, slurring her words, sounding tired.

Shawn noticed all signs of his organizing had disappeared. Her books were spread across the floor, clothes were strewn across the chairs, a few broken dishes littered the floor. There was no sign of her dog. "Where's Barney?"

"Safe in a new home."

"Why? How did everything get so messy?" Shawn flipped on the lamp next to her bed and saw Violet clearly for the first time. Her left eye was purple and swollen. Her face was pale and damp. Her eyes were open but drained of energy. He gasped and his skin tingled. "What happened?"

Violet pointed to her eye. "A wedding gift. From Anton."

Shawn grew hot with anger. He whipped out his phone. "I'm calling the police."

Violet shook her head. "No, please. The police put girls like me behind bars, not the guys who pimp us. Then Anton would make me pay for that. The other girls too."

Shawn slowly returned his phone to his pocket. That dark, hopeless feeling roared back. "I have almost half. Do you think he'll take it?"

She looked up to him with glistening eyes and looked genuinely touched. "That's sweet." She pulled the covers closer to her neck. "But even if you had it all, he'd just raise the price again. He'd kill me before he let me go. I overheard him talking to a gang member about moving us. I'm just glad I could see you before he did."

"You can't give up." Shawn wrung his hands. "Come back to my grandma's home."

"That's the first place he'd look. And I don't think she'll put out her welcome mat," she said with a wry look.

"My brother's place, then."

"Girls have tried to get away from him before," she said with a strained voice. "He works with other gangs. They track women down. Then they go missing." She reached into her purse and pulled out her pillbox with a trembling hand.

"You take those a lot. Are they good for you?"

Violet shook her head.

"I can get rid of them," Shawn said, holding out his hand for the case.

Violet turned her head to the side. "I'm really hurting."

Shawn placed his hand on hers. It felt electric, but he kept it there. "We can get through this together. I threw out a big box of doughnuts for Grandma when she was trying to lose weight."

She reluctantly handed him her pills. Shawn walked them over to the sink and poured them down the drain. "We should get you to the hospital."

"You should leave before he comes back."

"Not without you."

"You think I look bad now? I found Barney a new home so Anton can't hurt him again." Her eyes filled with tears. "You have to leave now, for good."

Shawn shook his head. He reached out, took her hand, and gazed into her eyes. "I couldn't hold anyone's hand for long before I met you. I never wanted to."

"As long as he thinks we're together, he'll know how to find me."

Shawn thought for a moment. "Then we'll have to convince him we're not together."

Violet furrowed her brows. "How would we do that?"

Shawn took a moment. "I don't know. We'd have to make it look like we broke up."

Violet sat up in bed. "You said you're not good at pretend."

"I'm a bad liar."

Violet smiled. "You know what? It's just acting. I'll direct you through it. We'll have to put on a show. Make it convincing. I'll slap you—"

"Too painful. Can't handle pain."

"I'll pretend to slap you. Pretend."

Shawn gave her a doubtful look and could feel his hands sweating. Maybe this wasn't such a good idea after all. But he knew deep down he would have to make this work. Their future depended on it.

# CHAPTER 19

# A BIG MISTAKE

Shawn and Violet worked out the details of their fight and exited Violet's building to debut their show. Across the street, Anton talked on his cell phone while eyeing his women. Aleesha and Natasha stood on either side of him, waving at oncoming cars and strutting down the sidewalk. A few cars honked. Most of them passed them by. They were only outside on nights when online demand was slow.

Violet turned to Shawn. "Ready?" He nodded and gave her a thumbs up.

They hurried away from the building toward the steps that emptied onto the sidewalk below. Shawn grabbed Violet's arm and pulled her down the stairs. She yelled loud enough for Anton to hear. "Get off me!"

"Shut up!" Shawn screamed back, trying not to laugh. It felt so weird for him to say something he didn't mean. He did his best to hide his smile as he pulled her down the steps.

Violet narrowed her eyes onto Shawn. "Don't you get it? It was all a lie. You think I care about you? You were just another john." She pretended to slap him across his face. He held his face as if she hurt him. Then she pushed him away. He played along, his smile breaking through.

"I love you," Shawn said.

Violet scoffed. "You don't know what love is. And I'm done selling mine to you."

"You don't mean that," he said in a hurt voice.

"I never want to see your face again," she shouted, giving him another fake slap.

Shawn cradled his shaking head in his hands. "I don't understand."

Violet jerked away from him. "Yeah, you do. Now go!"

They reached the bottom of the stairs and stepped onto the sidewalk. Violet pretended to knee Shawn in his stomach, just like they rehearsed. He hunched over and let out a fake moan.

"Get outta here!" Violet shouted.

Shawn straightened up and looked her deep in her eyes. "I made a big mistake with you."

He winked at her, happy with their work. Neither of them realized Anton had darted over to them in the middle of their fight. As Shawn turned to leave, he caught a glimpse of Anton, who punched him in his stomach.

Shawn doubled over, his body screamed with pain. Anton struck Shawn again in his side. A crippling sting ripped through Shawn, and he collapsed onto the sidewalk. Tears gushed down his face and blurred his vision.

"You bothering my sweetie?" Anton yelled.

Violet cringed at the sight of Shawn lying helpless on the sidewalk. "I told him to leave. It's over between us. For good."

Anton towered over Shawn, cracking his knuckles. "You got my fifteen thousand, pal?" Shawn shook his head, his whole body trembling. Anton scowled. "Then it's bye-bye to your babe." Anton swiftly kicked Shawn in his gut. Shawn screamed, and his body hummed with pain.

"He gets it," Violet said, fingering her necklace.

Anton jabbed a finger in Shawn's face and shouted in his ear. "Do you? Do you get the message?" Anton's lips pulled back, revealing a menacing smile. Then, he pummeled Shawn. Violet stepped forward and reached for Anton but caught Shawn's glance. He painfully shook his head, warning her to stay back as Anton laid into him. Shawn knew he was earning her freedom.

"Feels like I'm beating up a kid. You're making me feel bad," Anton said between blows.

Shawn was desperate for Anton to stop hitting him, but he didn't know how to make him quit. He reached into his pockets with shaking hands and pulled out the hundred-dollar bills. Anton grabbed them. "What's this? A going-away present? I'll take it. Now go away."

Anton kicked Shawn in his face. Shawn convulsed. His whole body throbbed with a new depth of pain. He was woozy and breathing hard. Anton grabbed Violet and ran his calloused fingers through her hair. "You know I'll protect you no matter what, honey. Now get upstairs. Got a guy coming over who doesn't care what you look like. Just wants it dark. No faces. Anonymous."

Violet coughed. "I'm still sick. I need a doctor or something."

Anton glared at her. "I tell you what you need. Get your freakin' lights off, and I'll bring him up." When Anton nearly swore, Violet knew he was on the brink of hurting her. He watched his language around them so he could pretend to be a nice guy, but there was always a vicious tiger lurking underneath.

"Five minutes," Anton said.

Violet nodded. She ran up the stairs toward her apartment while Anton turned to wave down a cab. Violet glanced back to Shawn, then hurried toward the front doors.

A taxi pulled up to the curb. Anton opened the back door and hoisted Shawn onto the backseat. He peeled off several bills and handed them to the cabbie.

"Got mugged. He'll be fine. Take him to Central Park West and 72nd."

Shawn's heartbeat pounded in his ears. He turned to Anton. "I wish I never met her." Anton laughed and slammed the door. The cabbie pulled away.

"You really okay?" the cab driver asked Shawn as he drove down Pennsylvania Avenue. Shawn could taste blood trickling into his mouth. He couldn't speak.

Violet rushed into her apartment and slammed the door. *How could Anton hurt Shawn like that? And how could Shawn take all that pain?* Her body started shaking uncontrollably. She sobbed and wiped the tears from her eyes.

She looked around and realized she was taking too long. Anton had her on a short leash. She doubted she could ever get away from him. *Was everything Shawn did for nothing?* She folded her hands as she paced and prayed a desperate prayer. I need help. A miracle. Violet pulled a pen out of her purse and wrote Anton a note: *Went to the hospital.*

She stuffed a few pictures and clothes into her large purse and picked up Theo the bear. Then she realized he was too big and returned him to the dresser next to her bed. She stuck her hand into its stuffing to search for bills but realized time was running out. Anton could be there any moment. She was only able to pull out a few dollars. Taking a deep breath, she forced herself out the door.

Rushing down the hallway, Violet avoided the elevator in case Anton was already on the hunt for her. She fled down the stairs and arrived at the first floor. She quietly opened the door and peered into the hallway. No sign of Anton. Violet hurried to the entrance and looked through the glass doors. Still no sign.

She slid through the front door and peered around the corner of the building. Anton was busy talking to his girls. Aleesha caught sight of Violet and looked like she was about to yell out, but Violet frantically shook her head not to. Aleesha got the hint. Instead, she turned back to Anton and kept his attention.

Violet rushed down the steps, then made her way down the sidewalk. She didn't dare look across the street again as she hurried away from her apartment and her life. Blocks away, she hid next to a dumpster and pulled out her phone, dialing Shawn.

"Are you okay?" Violet asked.

"Are you?" Shawn asked back.

"You're the one who got beat up."

There was a pause. "You're worth it," Shawn said.

A cozy feeling washed over Violet. She wasn't used to people talking to her that way. She could hear a lot of chatter and beeping on the other end of the phone.

"Where are you?" Violet asked.

"In a cab on the way to Mount Sinai Hospital," Shawn said.

Violet wiped a tear off her cheek. "I'll be right there."

She smashed her phone against the sidewalk and threw the pieces into the dumpster.

Shawn followed the path of the doctor's penlight with his eyes, then was X-rayed, poked, and prodded. Violet told him his swollen lips gave him all the benefits of a lip injection without the cost. The doctor assured Shawn his lips would return to normal. They took a taxi back to Ruth's apartment and avoided Douglas as they made their way to the elevator.

Then, they waited for Ruth to return.

An hour later, the apartment door opened, and Ruth stepped inside, Bible in hand. She saw Shawn sitting next to Violet on the couch. They both looked like they were on the losing end of a boxing match.

Ruth winced and rushed over to them. "Tell me what happened."

They started to talk but stopped. Shawn didn't know where to begin. He gave Ruth a wry look. "I wondered what Violet saw in her pimp. Then it hit me." He mimicked a hand punching his face and grinned. Ruth did not.

Violet slowly smiled. "A joke. A well-timed joke." Shawn and Violet both laughed painfully, unable to stop themselves. Violet turned to Shawn. "Look at the colors on my face. What do you hear?"

"Eeeeeeeeeeek," Shawn said. They laughed hysterically. They were losing it.

"Hey, Grandma, I won my wife back after all. How'd I do it? Beats me!" Shawn slapped his knee.

"And for half price," Violet added. They high fived each other. Shawn grimaced from the pain, but that didn't keep him from laughing and laughing until his smile started to fade as reality returned.

Ruth folded her arms. "You've clearly suffered brain damage."

As their laughing dwindled, Shawn felt tears running down his cheeks. He glanced over to Violet, who wiped tears from her eyes. Shawn pulled her toward him so she could nestle against his chest. As he felt the warmth of her body, Shawn could feel the torment of what happened begin to ebb. Ruth watched them embrace, her eyes filled with amazement at seeing Shawn holding someone for that long. After a moment, Ruth hurried into the kitchen, where she grabbed a first aid kit from underneath the sink.

Shawn waved his hand. "We've been to the hospital. I'll be okay."

"You don't look okay. Have you told the police?" Ruth asked.

Violet spoke up quickly. "We did everything we could."

Ruth studied Violet with a pinched expression that managed to seem both worried and irritated at the same time. "Shawn, please go to the bathroom and wet a washcloth."

"I can do it," Violet said, standing up.

Ruth motioned for Violet to sit back down with a stern look. Shawn got to his feet and carefully limped down the hallway, obviously in pain. When he was out of earshot, Ruth leaned close to Violet. "Ten thousand dollars is yours. If you leave my grandson and the city and never come back."

Violet peered at Ruth, looking like she was thinking this through. She clenched her jaw and slowly shook her head. Ruth started to breathe rapidly as if an attack was coming on.

Ruth fixed her eyes on Violet. "I heard you want to go to NYU," she said between breaths. "What's their school color? That's right. Violet. Would Violet like to be a violet? You just have to leave my grandson for good." Ruth controlled her breathing as she waited for Violet to answer.

Violet spoke in a steady, lower-pitched voice. "I know marriage won't be easy. But we're in this together."

Ruth gave Violet a curt nod. "If anything happens to me, I'll put Shawn into a facility where they'll help him get by. He'll be taken care of."

"We're going to take care of each other."

Ruth studied Violet. "You don't have to."

Violet stood up. "Good. Because I want to. That's what you do when you love someone," she said, raising her voice.

Sunny and Cloudy chirped from their cage in the corner of the room.

Ruth crossed her arms. "You woke up my birds."

"They're not the only love birds here."

Ruth looked Violet up and down as if she were trying to figure her out. "Twenty thousand."

Violet took a moment and looked Ruth in her eyes. "I once thought I wanted your money. But then I realized my husband is priceless."

Ruth wiped a tear from her eyes and looked away from Violet as if she was embarrassed.

Violet slid the rings off her finger. "I know you want these back."

Ruth took back the rings and looked surprised by the gesture. Her breathing returned to normal. Shawn returned with the washcloth and handed it to Ruth, who didn't seem to know what to do with it.

"Is it okay for Violet to stay here tonight?" Shawn asked.

Ruth looked between Shawn and Violet and stretched the silence until she couldn't lengthen it anymore. Ruth's cellphone rang, and she answered it. "Hello, Douglas. It's rather late." She paused and listened. Then she turned to Violet and Shawn. "Someone's here to see you." Ruth spoke into the phone. "What's the name again?" She muffled the receiver. "Anton."

Shawn's stomach bottomed out, and the blood in his veins turned to ice. Violet gripped his arm tight. Shawn wrung his hands and rocked back and forth. Ruth's face softened. She spoke into the phone. "We're not having any visitors tonight, Douglas. Please show him out." Ruth hung up the phone. "Who is Anton?"

Shawn rushed past Ruth and locked the front door. "Violet needs to stay here tonight."

"I'm getting worried," Ruth said. "This is exactly why I didn't want you to get involved with her."

"Too late for that, Grandma." Shawn said, feeling his face flush with anger. "We just need to figure some things out."

Ruth looked into his eyes and nodded. "You can sleep here tonight. But tonight only."

Shawn took the wet washcloth from his grandma and carefully placed it on Violet's forehead. He took her hand and led her down the hallway into his room.

# CHAPTER 20

## I KNOW THE FUTURE

Shawn led Violet into his bedroom, turned on the light, and shut the door. He turned to her, his face filled with worry. "We have to go to the police."

Violet shrugged and shook her head. "I don't know what they could do. When I moved here, I didn't have any money. Anton took care of everything. He'll say I was paying him back."

"Most people get jobs to pay off debts."

Violet looked out Shawn's window and wrapped her arms around herself. "That was my job."

Shawn opened his mouth to say something but couldn't find the right words. He knew what she was saying wasn't right. "You don't pay someone back with your body."

"You think I wanted to?" Violet looked into his eyes as if she wanted to tell him something. She started to talk but stopped herself. Squeezed her eyes shut. She took his hand and led him over to the bed where they sat across from each other. "My debt started soon after Anton took me in. I met him while I was looking for cheap Broadway tickets at that kiosk in Times Square. Anton told me he'd never seen someone as gorgeous as me. He wouldn't stop telling me how beautiful I was."

"You are beautiful," Shawn said.

She smiled. "I didn't feel that way on the inside. Anton took me to dinners, to shows, and bought me little gifts and jewelry for no reason at all. He made me feel special. No one had ever treated me that way before. He called me his girl, and I called him my lover boy."

Violet explained how they were inseparable. Anton paid for her to get an apartment when she couldn't afford one on her own. Then he made sure her refrigerator was full, and she had nice clothes hanging in her closet. His taste was more daring than hers. Anton liked to buy her tight dresses and fancy stilettos she would never buy herself. Whenever Violet told Anton she felt indebted to him, he would grin and tell her there was nothing he wouldn't do for her.

One Saturday, he took her out for breakfast and talked about his friend Joe as he dipped his bacon into the runny eggs on his plate. "I owe him a big favor. I thought you could help me pay him back."

Violet spread strawberry jam on her toast. "Just let me know how I can help."

Anton caressed her arm. "You could go on a date with Joe."

She looked up to him with a grin, thinking he was joking.

"Just one night," Anton said.

Violet shook her head and tilted her head to the side. "Honey, I'm your lover."

"Baby, I know. You'd just be on loan for the night. Not a big deal."

She put down her toast and suddenly didn't feel hungry anymore. "On loan? I'm not a library book."

Anton shrugged. "Honey I wouldn't ask if it wasn't a huge deal. I'm in debt to this guy, and he gets lonely."

"That's not my problem," Violet said.

Anton slid back in his chair. "You're right. It's not. Nothing's a problem for you. I make sure of that."

Violet reached out for Anton, but he pulled away. "You know I appreciate you."

"No, I get it. I never should've asked you. I'm sorry, baby. I'll come up with something else." Anton pulled a couple twenties out of his pocket and flung them onto the table. Violet peered into his eyes and smiled, waiting for him to smile back. He looked away. She fingered her diamond bracelet and could feel her chest tighten. *How could he even suggest something like that? I'm his girl. Not anyone else's.* She suddenly felt cheap, as if she was just a piece of property for him. Shaking her head, she dismissed her feelings. She was obviously being too sensitive.

On their way back to her apartment, Anton walked briskly, and she raced to keep up. She wasn't used to him acting this way and it made her uneasy. He was the only reason she wasn't on the streets. A week later, he brought over some Chinese takeout, and they watched a movie on his laptop from her couch.

"I need to get you a real TV," Anton said.

"You've been good enough to me," Violet said.

He kissed the back of her neck. "Nothing's too good for my baby."

He ran his fingers through her hair and leaned up against her. "I still feel stupid about my friend Joe."

"Don't feel that way," Violet said.

"He lent me money when I needed it. He was a real friend."

Violet popped a wonton into her mouth. "Well, let me know if there's anything else I can do."

Anton looked up. "He did say something about having dinner with us."

"Why would he care about dinner with me?" Violet asked.

"I guess I go on and on about you too much. Joe wanted to meet you."

"Well, if you want us to have dinner with him, go ahead and set that up," Violet said, scooping more noodles onto her plate. Something about the request still made her feel uneasy but she didn't know why.

The next day, Anton texted her the address and room number at an upscale hotel in Brooklyn and told her to wear something cute. She waited for Anton in front of the hotel, but he didn't show up. She finally got a text from him that said he was running late, and she should meet Joe at his hotel room. He'd join them there.

She took the elevator to the third floor and found Joe's room. She knocked and he was quick to open the door. Joe was in his forties, had a jowly face, rough hands and some gray hair that fanned away from his temples.

"Here," Joe said, handing her a glass of red wine. "There's some cheese on the table. I'm still getting ready."

"I can wait for dinner," Violet said, swishing the wine around the glass.

"That's too expensive to waste," Joe said as he buttoned up his white shirt. He wore jeans and seemed underdressed for a night on the town. Violet sipped the wine. It tasted fruity but had a bitter undertaste. "You finish that, and we can get moving." Joe said as he rolled up his sleeves.

Violet threw back her head and finished off the wine. Since she entered his room, an uneasy feeling enveloped her. She wanted to get out of there as soon as possible. Something about Joe didn't strike her right. It was his eyes. There was something dark and hollow about them.

Violet touched her head. She felt strange and tingly. Light. Euphoric. The floor seemed to warp in front of her eyes. She looked up, and Joe was upon her, pushing her toward the bed. She lost her balance and fell backward while he pressed himself against her. She yelled out. His sweaty hands muffled her screams as he pushed her into the bed. She kicked at Joe and tried to grab his hair. He grabbed her arms and pinned her against the bed. She didn't know if she was going to live or die. Her breath became ragged, and her head ached. The room spun. Then everything went black.

Violet fluttered her eyes open. She lay on the cold white tile floor of the bathroom, groggy and naked. Her body felt sore all over. Stumbling to her feet, she grabbed the edge of the sink to steady her balance. She pulled a white towel off the rack and wrapped it around herself.

She heard Joe's voice from the other room. She limped into the bedroom, where Joe sat on the edge of the bed, talking on his cell phone as if nothing had happened. He muted the phone and motioned to the door. "Get the hell out."

Violet's stomach twisted as rage surged through her veins. She rushed at Joe, but he rose to his feet as if expecting her. He kneed her in the stomach and shoved her down to the floor. She fell onto her knees, tears streaming down her cheeks.

Joe kicked her clothes over to her. "I'm not asking again."

Violet opened her mouth to say something but stopped herself. She quickly pulled on her dress and grabbed her purse. Violet opened the door. As she stepped out, Joe shoved her into the hallway and latched the door behind her. Violet stood there sobbing, unsure what to do. She pulled her phone out of her purse and called Anton.

"Baby? Where are you?" Anton asked.

She struggled to get the words out. "I'm… I'm at the hotel. He…he hurt me."

"What? I'm nearby. I'll meet you out front," Anton said.

Violet hung up, hobbled over to the elevator, and rode it down. She felt a rush of cool air as the elevator doors opened in the lobby. Violet hurried outside, where Anton waited in his blinged-out Range Rover. She ducked inside.

Violet smacked Anton with her purse. "Where were you?" He grabbed her arm and pushed her away, peeling down the street and around the corner. He squealed the car to a halt in the alley behind a building.

"Do that again, you lose a hand," he yelled, his face flush with anger.

"Your friend raped me," Violet said through tears.

Anton locked the doors. "Calm down. You were just helping me out."

"Helping you out? I said he raped me."

"I heard what you said."

All the blood rushed to Violet's head. Her eyes opened with disbelief.

Anton reached into his pocket and pulled out a wad of hundred-dollar bills. He fanned through them. "Not only did you make me even. He liked you." Violet felt like her heart was about to explode. "Joe feels bad he got carried away. But he wouldn't stop talking about how good you were."

"He drugged me. I blacked out."

"It got out of hand. All right? But it's over. Whatever you did, you did right." He grabbed her hand and rubbed it across the cash. She jerked her hand away and stared out the window. She wanted it all to go away.

"Here," Anton said, handing her a pill.

"What's that?"

"Just something to take the edge off," Anton said. She took the pill and looked it over. Anton caressed the back of her head. She slipped the pill into her mouth and swallowed, hoping it would mute the pain. In a few moments, she felt a strange tingling that numbed her and gave her a sense that everything would be okay.

Anton put the car into gear and started driving. "When you feel better, I've got another friend you can see."

"I don't want to see another friend," Violet said, sinking into her seat as a sweet feeling engulfed her.

"This is how you can pay me back," Anton said.

"That's not funny. I just want to go home before this wears off," Violet said.

Anton brought Violet back to her apartment and helped her into her shower. The hot water felt better than it ever had before. As she dried off, Anton waited, checking his phone.

"I don't want to keep this guy waiting," Anton said. "You'll make even more with this one."

"You need to stop. I'm going to sleep," Violet said, heading toward her bed. "Then we're gonna talk to the police."

Anton stepped in her way. "It won't take long."

Violet shook her head. Anton held up his phone screen. She squinted her eyes to get a better look. The pics on his phone were pornographic.

"Don't show me that," Violet said with disgust, turning her eyes away.

Anton motioned to the pics. "That's you, baby."

Violet grabbed his phone and looked at the pictures. He was right. Joe was in the shots too. She scrolled through the pics. Each one got worse and worse. A feeling of horror erupted from the pit of her stomach and clawed at her heart.

Anton grabbed the phone from her. "I don't want to post these anywhere. I'd hate for your mom or dad to see them. Or people you know back home in Jersey." He looked her over. "You want people to see you this way?"

Violet shook her head and wrapped her arms around herself. A deep feeling of shame swallowed her whole.

"Here," Anton said, handing her another pill. She swallowed it quickly. "There's a bright side to all this. We get to be in business together. You get to pay me back, I'll keep a roof over your head, pretty things on that hot body of yours."

Violet felt trapped. Confused. Angry. She hadn't worked at a real job for a while and relied on Anton to get by. She didn't have any of her own money. She needed the apartment and all the ways he provided for her.

Anton took her to meet a man that night who was just as nervous as she was. She went through the motions as if this was normal for her, but she could feel herself sinking into despair. There was another man after that, and another. She hated what she was doing but pushed it out of her mind.

Anton kept giving her pills which made it more bearable, while he told her how much he cared about her. He explained how he'd make sure she was always okay and would give her a share of their profits.

"I don't want profits. I want this to stop," Violet said.

"I'm afraid you stopping means you stop for good. You get what I'm saying?"

Violet shook her head. "Stop it with the threats."

"This isn't a threat. It's your new reality. It's a dangerous world out there. Parents get killed, friends get killed, and no one ever knows."

Violet held out her hand for another pill, and he gave it to her. She told Anton she would keep going but only until she paid him off and could get back on her feet.

"Sure, baby," he said.

The pills helped Violet get through the nights. But each time she took one, that euphoric feeling seemed to get further and further out of her reach. When Violet refused to do what Anton said, he would hit her and then apologize, telling her she gave him no other choice and promising he'd be different next time. He threatened Violet and her family until she learned to fall in line.

She kept telling herself this wouldn't last forever, and now and then he'd say to her how close she was to paying off her debt to keep her going. But then something costly would happen. She'd get arrested for solicitation, or she'd need to see a doctor. She began to realize the debt she owed would continue to balloon unless she was careful and took better care of herself.

She started cutting back on the drugs. Now she only needed a pill now and then to get through the night or deal with memories when they began to haunt her. She took up baking but mostly gave away what she created to her neighbors so she wouldn't put on weight. She wanted to start painting again but never got around to it.

Violet wiped her eyes as she told her story to Shawn. "Joe was never just a friend. I found out later that was a service he did for gangs."

"That's evil. Completely evil," Shawn said. "I'm so sorry."

"That's the first time I told someone everything." Violet's whole body trembled as tears ran down her cheeks. Shawn opened his arms and embraced her. They held each other for a long time. Violet dabbed the tears from her face. "We should think about our future now. I'm finally free."

A sense of dread snaked through Shawn's mind. "But Anton knows where I live. And maybe we should think about the future of the other women too."

Violet pulled back from him. "I know the future I want to have, and it's right here. With you."

Shawn nodded. "It is for me too. But I don't think we can both fit on my twin bed."

Violet laughed. "You're right. I'll take the floor."

Shawn smiled. "Of course not. I'm pretty sure there are still ants down there. You take my bed."

"You're still recovering."

"You're my wife. My wife doesn't sleep on the floor." Shawn folded his comforter to create a cushion for himself next to his bed. "I appreciate you sharing your story. We'll figure out a way to get Anton away from us."

"Thanks for being such a good listener." They were both so

exhausted, they lay down and were immediately fast asleep.

Outside Shawn's door, Ruth wiped tears from her own eyes. On the way to her bedroom, she had heard them talking and stopped to listen in. Ruth told herself it was her home, and she had the right to listen to what was going on. But now she felt terrible because she knew Violet's whole story but couldn't let them know. She carefully stepped down the hall to go to bed.

Ruth woke up the next morning and googled "how to help a prostitute" on her phone. It was the least she could do. Then Ruth hurried over to the kitchen and prepared Shawn's daily oatmeal with an extra serving for Violet. She turned on the coffee maker since that's what a good host would do. Ruth then slipped back into her bedroom to give them privacy and look at what her phone discovered. Shawn always told her she could look at her search results right away, but she liked to give her phone some time so it could get the job done right.

Shawn woke up to the smell of his favorite apple cinnamon oatmeal. As he sat up, his back ached from sleeping on the floor, but he didn't mind the pain when he saw Violet curled up on his bed.

Shawn was delighted to see his grandma had made an extra serving and decided to wait for Violet to join him as long as it didn't take her too long. The coffeemaker was also on which was strange because Shawn never drank coffee. He searched his phone for ideas that could help them.

Violet trudged down the hallway and smiled at seeing Shawn. "Ooooh. Coffee." She poured herself a cup and plopped down at the dining room table across from Shawn. "After everything I talked about, you're still here."

"Of course I am," Shawn said. "Do you want to pray for our food?"

"You can do that."

"It's really easy. You just thank God for it and ask him to bless the day."

Violet picked up her coffee mug. "Well, I'm glad for this. That's for sure." She looked up. "Thanks, God." It wasn't what Shawn was expecting but he didn't mind. He picked up his spoon and started eating.

"Turns out the police have a special unit that helps with human trafficking cases," he said.

Violet gave a half-hearted shrug. "I was paying a debt."

Shawn read his phone. "Human trafficking is the trade of humans, most commonly for sexual slavery, forced labor, or commercial sexual exploitation."

Violet looked up. "Thank you, Mr. Google."

Ruth stepped into the room in an elegant robe, holding her phone. "Anton is downstairs."

Violet stood up. "I'll talk to him."

Shawn pushed away from the table. "I can't let you do that."

"He'll never leave us alone," Violet said.

Shawn pointed to his bruised face. "This is how he communicates."

Ruth put the phone back to her ear. "Douglas, please make him go away." Ruth hung up her phone and placed a piece of paper on the table in front of Violet. "You can send a text to that place to get help. Looks like they offer rehab and other services." Violet looked over the piece of paper, exchanging glances with Shawn. "Your pajamas look a lot like what you wore yesterday," Ruth said. "I might have something you can wear."

"I need to pick up a few things back at my place," Violet said.

Shawn looked at her with concern. "You can't go back there." He knew if she weren't careful, she'd endanger her life and their future.

Violet folded her arms. "I'm tired of Anton controlling me."

# CHAPTER 21

# A RARE TALENT

Violet stepped out of a cab in front of her old apartment building with a large empty bag slung over her shoulder. It had been a few days, but she knew she had to return. Too much of her history still lived there, and Violet didn't want Anton throwing it out. Glancing around, she didn't see any signs of him. He was likely recovering from the night before. She started walking up the stairs.

"Haven't seen you around." Violet's body tensed. She looked up to see Goldie sitting at the top of the steps, holding a bottle enrobed in a paper bag. Goldie grinned at her, gold teeth shining, still dressed in a heavy wool coat with a leopard print, despite it being a hot day. "People been asking about you, sugar."

Violet stomped up the steps on a mission. "Well, you can tell people I've moved on."

"Must be nice," Goldie said, taking a swig. Her eyes bore down on Violet. "Heard you're living fancy now. Hope it lasts."

"I know you're one of his spies," Violet said. "I just need a few minutes."

Goldie grinned. "It's just business."

Violet shook her head as she stepped past her, over to the entrance of the building. She punched in the door code and rode the elevator up to her floor. As the elevator doors opened, her stomach churned. She didn't want to be there, but she knew she couldn't stay away. Anton wasn't going to have the last word on what she did with her life.

She carefully unlocked her apartment door and slipped inside, not sure what would still be there.

Everything looked exactly how she left it. A mess. She shut the door quietly and let out a sigh of relief. She spotted her NYU bear Theo and hugged him. Then she found her diary and the pictures of her family and stuffed them into her bag.

Her door burst open. A tingling rush of fear swept through Violet. Anton marched inside, dressed in an athletic suit, biting the final bits of flesh off a chicken wing. He slammed the door and grinned at Violet as he tossed the wing into her sink.

"Look who slithered back in. Without even saying hello." Anton's words created a prickly, piercing feeling in Violet as if he were pressing a needle into her flesh.

"You don't own me anymore," Violet said.

"Of course I do." Anton licked the ends of his fingers. "And I've got a backlog of customers who can't wait to get a taste of you."

"I worked for you long enough. I'm moving on with my life."

"Sweetie, you can retire when you're dead." Anton picked up her bag and flipped it upside down, spilling everything onto the floor.

Violet grabbed the bag, knelt, and stuffed her belongings back inside.

"I've always treated you good. And that's never gonna end," Anton said. He pulled a bottle of pills out of his pocket and shook them. "I think you need a little pick-me-up."

Violet groaned. "You never give me enough pills to get through the whole night anymore."

"I got whatever you need. You want more? Something stronger? Done."

She finished putting everything in her bag and stood up. "Anton, you think too small."

"I've been talking to some boys in the 14th Street Gang. We're gonna partner up, so it's not just us anymore. They've got all kinds of connections and feel-good meds."

Violet pushed back her hair. "I don't like how you hold my debt over me."

"Oh, baby. I just do what I have to do. You know that." He caressed the back of her neck. "I'm all talk and just a little action. Only when you back me into a corner."

"What about Aleesha? Natasha? What's their debt?" Violet moved across the room to grab more things, but Anton followed like a cat to a mouse.

"They never had it so good. I'm only a daddy who keeps his kids in line."

"We're not your kids."

"I've always treated you like family." Anton returned to the door and leaned against it. "Now, you need to get yourself ready to join your sisters. I posted some new ads. Demand is gonna be high tonight. Don't mind me, sweetie." Anton pulled out a pocketknife and cleaned under his fingernails.

Violet's heart beat rapidly in her chest, and her throat tightened. She slowly put Theo the bear onto her bed. "You know why I came back here? To prove to myself that I'm free from you."

Anton laughed. "The only thing you proved is how stupid you are."

"I'm smarter than you think, sweetie." Violet unbuttoned her blouse, revealing a small microphone underneath.

"What the hell is that?"

The door burst open, sending Anton across the room. Police streamed into the apartment, guns drawn, shouting for Anton to drop the knife. He stood there, glaring at Violet. Then he let the knife fall with a thud onto the floor.

A burly officer pulled Anton's hands above his head.

"You've got any more weapons? Anything sharp? I don't want any surprises," the officer said. Anton shook his head, keeping his eyes fixed on Violet. The officer patted him down and pulled out a small bag of pills. He handed it to another officer who handcuffed Anton and read him his rights. Two others joined them to escort Anton down the hallway.

Once he was gone, Violet felt like she could breathe again. She looked around the mess of her apartment and wiped tears from her eyes. It was over. It was finally over. A female officer approached and put her hand on Violet's shoulder. "I'm sure that wasn't easy."

Violet nodded. "It just feels so hot in here."

"Let's get you outside." The officer motioned toward the door. Violet grabbed her bag and stuffed some more clothes and pictures inside. "We'll make sure you get everything," the officer said.

Violet grabbed Theo the bear and followed the officer down the hallway to the elevators where another police officer joined them. As they rode the elevator down, Violet thought about how strange it felt to share an elevator with two police officers when she'd spent most of her life avoiding them.

They stepped out of the building, and Violet knew she would never visit this part of New York City again. Someone touched Violet's shoulder. She turned to see Shawn standing there, looking concerned.

"Everything okay?" Shawn asked. Violet nodded. He wrapped his arms around her. "I'm proud of you," he whispered in her ear.

They held each other as more police officers and detectives poured into the apartment building. Anton watched them from the back of a nearby police car, his face taut with anger. Goldie watched from across the street, shaking her head.

Over the next month, Violet, Aleesha, and Natasha talked to the investigating detectives in the Brooklyn precinct. The police paired Violet with a female detective who asked her how she first met Anton and the events that led her to today.

The police discovered that Aleesha and Natasha were in the United States illegally, and Aleesha was also wanted for a couple of shoplifting charges. They were assigned lawyers who took up their cases with gusto. Aleesha and Natasha both appeared before a judge for a bail hearing. Shawn sat in the back of the courtroom next to Violet.

"They can't go to prison," Violet whispered.

"This is a special court designed for victims of human trafficking," Shawn said. "The judge will assess their situation and help get them into a program."

The judge asked Aleesha and Natasha about their journey to the United States. They both explained how they got trapped here and forced into prostitution when Anton took their passports and threatened to kill their families back home. The judge referred them to a drug treatment and rehab program while the lawyers helped them with their immigration status.

Aleesha called her family in Jamaica but didn't tell them all the details about what happened to her. They knew she had overstayed her tourist visa, and now the government was working out a way for her to stay in the country. Natasha got in touch with her dad in the city of Nizhny Tagil in Russia and told him the job opportunity she thought she was pursuing in the United States turned out to be something far worse. They wept together over the phone, and he promised to send her money so she could return as soon as possible. She told him she wanted to stay in New York City to get her life back together.

All three women testified in the case against Anton. His lawyers tried depicting him as a pimp with a heart of gold, despite what the women said about him.

Anton described himself as the head of a happy extended family working together for a brighter future. The prosecutor said Anton turned these women into his personal ATMs and urged the judge to give Anton the maximum sentence for preying on desperate young women and then brainwashing them. The jury found him guilty on all charges.

Anton was convicted of sex trafficking and sent to prison for fifteen years. He would have to register as a sex offender upon his release. Shawn didn't think that was enough time, and Violet agreed. Natasha and Aleesha joined an inpatient drug treatment program in New Jersey while Violet met one-on-one with an addiction medicine specialist in Manhattan. Shawn wanted her to stay close by. Violet met with the doctor each week, and he prescribed her medication that helped her deal with her withdrawal. She felt safe talking with her doctor about everything that happened to her. But still, Violet could hear Anton's voice inside of her, telling her that nothing was going to work out. She even wondered if she should visit Anton in prison to tell him what she thought of him. A tiny part of her still held feelings for him, though she couldn't understand why.

The end of the summer was nearing, and the weather began to cool. Shawn and his grandma took their usual trip to Redeemer Church one Sunday and, once again, Violet told them to go ahead without her. She didn't feel like church was yet the place for her.

Shawn left his Bible behind for Violet and suggested she read the book of John. He didn't know what else to say. During the taxi ride to the church, Shawn didn't feel like talking. He had hoped Violet would've joined them by now.

At church, the jazz quartet led the congregation through "Great Is Your Faithfulness" set to a contemporary beat. Great is your faithfulness, great is your faithfulness. Morning by morning new mercies I see; All I have needed your hand has provided. Great is your faithfulness, Lord, unto me.

Shawn sat beside Ruth and tried to keep up with the song, but his thoughts kept turning to Violet. He thought about all the prayers he had prayed in that church, for God to bring him someone special. Someone Shawn could share his life with. Someone he could love. Shawn found Violet, but now she wasn't by his side. He glanced at the back of the sanctuary and noticed Violet leaving through the rear doors. This was not his first sighting of her at church, but Violet rarely stayed until the end.

When they returned home, Shawn headed to his bedroom, which he now officially shared with Violet, ever since Ruth had gifted them a queen-size bed. Violet had changed out the curtains to something more modern and added a few colorful throw pillows. Theo the bear now enjoyed his new home on the desk next to the bobbleheads and games. A picture of Violet's face now smiled from the bride bobblehead. Painted scenes from the pages of Violet's diary decorated the walls. Ants scurried inside a new ant farm on the window sill.

Violet sat at the edge of their bed, folding clothes she pulled out of a wicker laundry basket. Shawn kissed her on her cheek. "I saw you at church. You're welcome to sit with us."

"I can only take parts of it for now. Between that and counseling, I feel like a walking wound. I feel terrible but also good at the same time. It's like I'm invisible, yet people see every inch of me."

Shawn tapped his finger against his bottom lip. "Will you sit by me next time?"

*You don't belong in a place like that*, Anton's voice said inside her mind. Violet looked down. "We'll see."

Shawn wanted to say more, but he also knew it was a good idea to give her space. That's what his grandmother recommended to him. He reached into his pocket and pulled out a diamond ring and a gold band. Violet looked them over. "That looks expensive."

"It's called a ziamond. It's fake, but I wanted you to wear something while I saved up for rings."

Violet slipped the rings onto her fingers. "Thank you."

There was a knock on their door. Shawn opened it to find Ruth standing there. "Your friends are here."

"What friends? Did you invite someone over?" Violet asked.

Shawn motioned for Violet to follow him. They stepped into the living room where Natasha and Aleesha stood in the doorway, dressed comfortably but looking out of place. Violet's face lit up, and she gave them both hugs. "What a surprise."

"We're out on a day pass," Aleesha said.

"From jail?" Ruth asked.

"No, grandma, from rehab. They're going to a program in New Jersey, remember?"

Ruth shrugged. "It's hard to keep track of all the details of your life."

Shawn pulled back one of the chairs from the table. "Please have a seat."

"What are you up to?" Violet asked as she took a seat next to Aleesha and Natasha. Ruth watched from the kitchen with a cautious look in her eyes. The doorbell rang.

"Can you get that, grandma?" Shawn asked.

Ruth opened the door to find Douglas holding several grocery bags. "I didn't order anything," Ruth said.

Shawn motioned for Douglas to come inside. "I did." Douglas carried the bags to the kitchen and pulled out several large pastry boxes.

"What's going on?" Ruth asked.

Shawn pulled a teapot out of the cabinet. "Scottish afternoon tea."

Douglas opened one of the boxes to reveal scones. Ruth shook her head in disapproval. "Well, those shouldn't be served from a box." Ruth grabbed a silver platter from the cabinet and a pair of tongs from the drawer next to her. She carefully arranged the scones on the tray.

Douglas picked up the tongs. "I can finish that. Maybe you can serve the cucumber sandwiches." He motioned to one of the boxes on the counter.

Ruth opened the box, and her eyes flickered with a look of delight as she eyed the tiny sandwiches inside. She thought for a moment, then opened another cabinet where she pulled out a three-tier silver serving stand. She stacked the sandwiches on the trays while Shawn turned on the burner underneath the teapot. "The electric kettle is a lot faster," Ruth said, pushing down the lever on the kettle next to her.

Douglas pulled a bouquet of colorful flowers out of one of the bags and handed them to Ruth. "These are for you."

"Thank you," Ruth said. She gave him a quick peck on his cheek.

Aleesha peered around at the room. "This place is like a museum."

"I wish I could paint like this," Violet said, looking at a painting of Central Park.

"Really?" Ruth asked. Violet nodded.

"I finally got me to the doctor," Natasha said.

"Yeah?" Aleesha asked.

Natasha nodded. "Got tired of it burning every time I peed."

Violet and Shawn exchanged glances.

Ruth brought the serving tray over to the table and set it up in the center. Douglas carried over the platter of scones.

"When are you two getting married for real?" Aleesha asked.

"We are married for real," Shawn said, bringing white teacups with gold trim over to the table.

Aleesha shook her head. "That was too quick a wedding. Not pretty. My girl likes to be treated special."

*Nothing's special about you*, Anton's voice said to Violet.

"I'm fine," Violet said. "Really."

Douglas poured hot water into a teacup and handed it to Ruth. She set it down on the table and pulled out the seat next to her. "Maybe you can spare some time away from the front desk?"

A smile of delight sneaked across Douglas' face. "My replacement arrived just before I came up."

"Oh, it's not easy to replace you," Ruth said, squeezing his arm. Douglas took a seat at the table. Shawn watched them talk in whispers while he handed out a tray filled with a variety of teas.

Violet nudged Shawn. "Thank you."

They took turns tasting the food around the table and sharing stories. Shawn couldn't remember the last time he had seen his grandmother laugh so much.

The next afternoon, Violet arrived back to the apartment after seeing her counselor. It was a grueling session where she unearthed more terrible memories. After she left her counselor, she wondered if she could ever truly move on. All her memories kept trying to drag her back down, and Anton's voice was always near.

Shawn hadn't returned from work, and Violet wanted to avoid questions from Ruth in case she was in a nosey mood. She headed down the hallway. Then she stopped and couldn't walk anymore. Her heart raced, and her feet felt heavy. Her hands trembled, then her arms, and her lips.

The reality of her life crashed over her like a waterfall. She leaned against the wall and sobbed. Tears gushed down her cheeks, too fast for her to wipe them away. Her heart wrenched, and she felt dizzy with sadness. She covered her face with her hands as her shoulders quaked. *Why?* She didn't have any answers. All the men she had been with flashed before her eyes in quick procession. She could smell their skin, their stale clothes, their breath laced with alcohol. It crushed her.

A hand holding a box of tissues appeared in front of Violet's face.

She looked up. Ruth patted her on the shoulder. "It'll get better," Ruth said.

"That's what my counselor keeps saying." Violet wiped the tears from her eyes.

"I've been praying for you."

"Thank you," Violet said. "I've never believed in prayer more than I do now."

"It's a beautiful day to paint," Ruth said.

"Oh, yes. Have a good time painting."

"I don't want to paint alone. Are you still interested in learning? Painting always helps me process through what's going on in my life."

*If you spend time with her, she'll know you're a fraud,* Anton's voice said.

Violet looked up, determined. "I'd like that very much."

Ruth grabbed a bag and packed easels and art supplies inside. They left the apartment and trekked across Central Park until they found a bench along a path bordered by trees. The smell of roasting cashews wafted through the air.

Ruth set up two easels and placed a canvas on each of them. Reaching into her bag, she pulled out a palette. She handed it to Violet and showed her how to hold it. Then Ruth pulled out paint tubes and squeezed different colors of paint onto the pallets.

"What should we paint?" Violet asked. Ruth pointed to the trees surrounding them. Grabbing a brush, Ruth painted a line down her canvas and motioned for Violet to draw a line down hers. She drew more lines and had Violet imitate her. After several more strokes, Violet could see trees emerge on her canvas.

Ruth glanced over to Violet's version of the trees. It was rougher, more childlike. Violet caught her looking and laughed at her amateur way of painting.

"I can see the passion you're putting into it," Ruth said. "It's a rare talent to be able to paint with your heart."

That Sunday, Shawn stepped out of a cab in front of Redeemer Church. The bruises on his face were healed but he still had a few scratches on his cheek. It had been a few months since Anton's arrest. Ruth exited the taxi after him, followed by Douglas. She reached out to grasp Douglas's hand and smiled as they walked past Shawn and entered the church. As a couple.

Watching them disappear inside the church, Shawn felt a tug of sadness on his heart as he thought about Violet. His shoulders slumped as he trudged toward the doors.

"Shawn!" He turned at hearing Violet's voice. She walked toward him, looking relaxed in a flowing wine-colored dress with small gray polka dots. Aleesha and Natasha were with her. "I hope you don't mind I brought some friends," Violet said.

"I couldn't be happier," Shawn said. "I'm just glad you didn't take them to your Holy Grail Church." Shawn winked and offered his hand. She took it. Together, they headed into church with Shawn leading the way. They found seats toward the back. Violet scooted in close to Shawn. She listened to a song about how God makes a way.

*God won't make a way for you,* Anton's voice said. She squeezed her eyes shut and prayed his condemning voice would stop.

# CHAPTER 22

## COLORS AND SOUNDS

A few weeks later, Shawn and Violet looked healthy and healed as they strolled through Shawn's former favorite dating spot, the High Line, under billows of clouds that dotted the blue sky. Shawn felt thankful those days were long gone. They walked next to a babbling stream of water, sharing a cup of sorbet.

Violet looked around. "You know what I like about this place? People thought it was worthless until someone realized it just needed a new start."

Shawn smiled. "That's what I like about it too." He wrung his hands and looked around as if he was nervous about something. "There's one thing I regret."

"What's that?"

"Our wedding wasn't as special as I always wanted it to be." Shawn kicked a rock in front of him.

"Yeah, I can see that." Violet imagined how disappointing that moment must have been for him after he bookmarked all those wedding websites and came up with a slew of ideas on what would make his perfect day. When she was young, she imagined what her wedding would be like but eventually filed those ideas in a folder labeled: impossible.

"And I bet you didn't feel that special either," Shawn said.

"That day felt like it happened ages ago."

He stopped walking and turned to her. Shawn reached for her hand and pulled off her rings.

"Hey, what are you doing?" Violet asked.

"You won't need these anymore." He tossed them into the trash can next to them.

Violet's face turned red. "I wanted those."

Shawn got down on one knee. "Would you marry me, Violet?"

Violet tugged on her ear. "I thought we were already married."

"Yes, or no?" Shawn asked.

Violet frowned. *What's he up to?* "Yes, of course."

Someone tapped Violet on her shoulder. She turned to see Aleesha and Natasha standing there, dressed sharply, as though they were going to a dinner party.

"Is she ready?" Aleesha asked Shawn.

"As ready as she'll ever be."

"Ready for what?" Violet asked.

"I hope you still like surprises," Shawn said.

Violet narrowed her eyes onto Shawn, wondering what was going on. Aleesha and Natasha took both her arms and led her to the stairs. She could feel butterflies bang up against the sides of her stomach. She looked back to Shawn, who wore a big goofy grin on his face. He was enjoying this.

Aleesha and Natasha walked Violet down the stairway, to a cab waiting on the street below the High Line. "I need a hint. Just a little hint," Violet said, but they both shook their heads.

All three of them slid into the back of the taxi. The driver took them to 10th Avenue and pulled up to an ancient cluster of red-brick buildings. A black sign stretched above the entrance read: The High Line Hotel.

Ruth waited for them at the curb, dressed in a flowing yellow dress. Violet opened the door, and Ruth took her hand to help her out. "Please tell me what's happening," Violet said.

Ruth didn't say anything and motioned to follow her into the tall brick building housing the hotel. "They believe the apple orchards on this land inspired New York City's Big Apple nickname back in the day," Ruth said.

Violet snickered. "You sound like Shawn."

They passed through the eclectic lobby with its cathedral ceilings bordered by exposed black beams. They continued down the hallway decorated with Victorian antiques, a mounted deer head, and landscape paintings covering the walls. A Tiffany-style lamp lit up the black and white zigzag-patterned couch. Violet was happy to realize she had never been to this hotel before. It was a little too hip for her clientele. She followed Ruth through a door at the side of the building while Aleesha and Natasha followed.

Violet stepped onto a patio decked out for a snazzy party. White tablecloths covered the tables with vases of wildflowers at their centers. A couple dozen women were seated, but Violet didn't recognize any of them. They smiled and clapped when Violet stepped over to them. Violet looked around, wondering who they were applauding. Then she realized it was her! She glanced around uneasily.

Then Violet saw Tammy, who rushed over to her, wearing a long green dress with a pin proclaiming: There is no Planet B. Tammy hugged Violet tight. "I brought a bunch of women from work," Tammy said, motioning to the younger women seated around the tables.

"And I filled in the rest," Ruth said, pointing to the older ladies with lived-in faces, who were mixed among them.

"I still don't know what's going on," Violet said. The ladies laughed.

"You never had a bridal shower," Ruth said, pointing to a decorated table against the brick wall.

A birdcage served as the centerpiece, filled with flowers with a sign above it, "Celebrating the Love Birds." Next to the cage was a tray of meatballs sprinkled with sesame seeds with a sign: 'Bird Seed Meatballs.' Sandwiches were named 'Lovebird Sandwiches.' Mini water bottles were labeled 'For Thirsty Birds.' Violet took a long, satisfying breath.

"I've never even been to a bridal shower," Violet said. "Just tell me what I should do." The women chuckled again.

"You don't belong here," a man said. Violet turned, then realized it was Anton's voice in her head. *These people don't know who you really are.*

"Just enjoy yourself," Ruth said as she ushered Violet to a seat at the center table, next to Tammy.

The next couple of hours were filled with the ladies giving Violet advice on marriage and relationships or confessing that things weren't so great in that department for themselves. "You have to choose to love each other, even when you don't feel like it. Some days you'll want to run the other way. That's when you remind yourself of your commitment," one of the older women said.

"And always answer your phone if he calls, but don't answer it when you're together," another woman said. The others nodded in agreement.

*And make sure you keep your secrets*, Anton said inside Violet's mind. *If he truly knows you, every part of you, you're doomed.*

"Be quick to admit when you're wrong," one of the younger women said. "That's helped my marriage a ton. And try to give your best to each other. Even after a crappy day. Make sure you budget for date nights. You've got to keep investing in your marriage for it to work."

*No one invests in a lost cause*, Anton's voice said. *I wasted plenty of time on you. Now it's Shawn's turn.*

Violet shook the thoughts from her head and looked up as a woman in her seventies stood up. "Find excuses to laugh," the woman said. "And remember, marriage isn't you doing fifty percent and him doing fifty percent. None of that fifty-fifty stuff. That only leads to divorce. Marriage is one hundred percent from you and one hundred percent from him. That's the only way it works

Violet nodded. *Your marriage will work as long as you keep being an actress. You know how to get what you want*, Anton's voice said. *Too bad that'll wear off soon. Then you'll realize you left the only thing you were good at: selling yourself.*

Violet crossed and uncrossed her legs. Her skin felt tingly while sweat formed along the rim of her neckline. Marriage sounded like a lot of work.

"And remember to pray together. God will give you the strength to love each other." It was Ruth talking this time. Violet gave her an appreciative smile.

A few more women talked, and Violet started to relax and enjoy the party. She kept thinking it was over until Ruth would announce something else they were going to do. They competed to be the first to complete a crossword puzzle, and all the words were about Violet and Shawn. They blindfolded themselves and guessed cake flavors, which Aleesha won. Then Tammy suggested Violet open the gifts stacked next to the door. After the first present was fancy pink lingerie, Ruth announced it would be more fun for Violet to open them in private.

As the guests started to trickle out, Violet overheard Tammy talking to Ruth. "What happened to the love birds I made?" Tammy asked her.

"What do you mean?" Ruth asked.

"I put them in the cage, but they're missing now, and the door is open."

"I took them out," Ruth said. "Because the real lovebirds are finally free." Violet beamed at the thought.

*You'll never be free*, Anton's voice said.

"Shut up," Violet said out loud and looked around, wondering if anyone heard her. She bowed her head and silently asked God to stop the condemning voices inside her head.

"This was a bad idea, wasn't it?" Colin asked Shawn as they stood inside the glass walls of The Press Lounge rooftop bar with its impressive panoramic views of the city from the bank of the Hudson River.

"It's a great bachelor party," Shawn said.

A handful of men from Shawn's work milled around the space, drinking beer and snacking from plates of appetizers. Since he arrived, Shawn had mostly stood in the corner next to the oval fireplace, wringing his hands.

"Everything okay?" Flynn asked as he stepped over, beer in hand.

Shawn nodded but didn't look him in his eyes.

"I think it's a lot for him," Colin said.

Flynn smiled. "Listen, man. It's an honor to be here. We all look up to you."

Shawn shook his head. "Please don't try to be funny."

"No, I'm not. You went for it. You really did. Nothing stopped you from finding the woman you wanted to spend the rest of your life with." Flynn tipped his glass to Shawn. "Here's to you." Flynn took a drink.

"But you could have anyone you want," Shawn said. "I see what you post online. You have an amazing life."

Flynn laughed. "Those are just pics. You're living in reality."

"Oh. Thanks, Flynn," Shawn said. He sat down on one of the brown leather couches. "I'm so worried I'm going to mess everything up. I can't even figure out what people are thinking half the time."

Colin whipped out his phone and pulled up an app. "This should help. Your favorite Bible verse. I waited patiently for the Lord; He turned to me and heard my cry."

Shawn closed his eyes for a moment. "Thank you."

Colin gestured to the other men in the room. "Anyone have any marriage or relationship advice for Shawn?"

An older man with graying hair that Shawn recognized from the finance department spoke up. "The best way to remember your wife's birthday is to forget it once." The others laughed. "Or any special event for that matter."

"Never go to bed angry," one of the guys said.

"Just stay up and fight all night." another man said. More chuckles.

"Always remember the three magic words," a stout man said that Shawn recognized from Think Coffee.

"I love you?" Shawn asked.

"Let's go out," the man said with a laugh. The men clinked their glasses.

"And never laugh at your wife's choices," Flynn said. "Because you were one of them."

"All right, all right," Colin said, handing Shawn a glass of iced tea. "I'd like to make a toast to my brother." He lifted his glass. "You're one of a kind, and so is your wife. I wish you lots of love and happiness together. I'll always be here for you, no matter what. And know that I love you."

The men clinked their glasses together. "Thank you," Shawn said.

"If you still want free coffee, I'll have to give it to you from the teachers' lounge," Colin said.

"You're serious?" Shawn asked.

Colin nodded. "And I asked Laura out on a date."

Shawn's eyes went wide. "Really?"

Colin nodded, then shook his head. "She said no."

"Don't give up so easily," Shawn said with a wink.

Colin clinked his glass with Shawn's. "You taught me that."

The final guests left Violet's party and waved goodbye. "See you soon," more than one of them said.

Violet turned to Ruth. "People keep saying they'll see me soon. Is there more to this?"

Ruth nodded. "You bet there is." She motioned to Aleesha and Natasha. "Ready?"

They both smiled and nodded. Ruth gestured for them to follow her. She led them back through the hallway to the elevators. Violet's heart fluttered as they waited for it to arrive. The day had already been overwhelming. She couldn't imagine what was in store next. The elevator arrived, and the doors opened. They rode it up to the fifth floor, where Ruth led them down the hallway to one of the rooms.

Inside, a slender young man with wavy hair, wearing a giant hoop earring and holding a hairdryer as though he was ready to get into a gunfight, shared a laugh with a petite woman with a handsome face and tanned skin. Ruth cleared her throat and won their attention.

The young man turned to greet Violet. "Are you ready?" he asked her.

"For what?"

The man laughed and put his hand on his hip. "Your wedding."

Violet turned to Ruth, who nodded and handed her a white terry cloth robe and a towel. "Once you're done with your shower, they'll get to work." Over the next several hours, they fussed over Violet's hair, nails, makeup, and more in a way she had never experienced before. She kept hearing Anton's voice tell her she didn't deserve any of this and prayed God would drown out his voice for good.

When the sky pinkened with dusk, Shawn stood ready in a classy black tuxedo with his bow tie finally tied perfectly. Colin waited with him, also in a tux. The lanky pastor next to them gave Shawn a nod. They stood on a small platform in front of a wooden arbor decorated with violets set against large glass panels that overlooked the traffic racing along 8th Avenue below. This was a popular spot for people on the High Line, but now it was reserved for only them.

A crowd of people sat on the wooden benches that sloped down to the platform, including Tammy, Flynn, Ruth's friends, and others from Shawn's work. Ruth sat in the front row with Douglas at her side, holding hands. Jake had declined his invitation, saying he had something else that afternoon. He didn't want to be there as an awkward reminder of Violet's past. Instead, he paid for all the flowers. Anonymously.

"Big moment," Colin whispered.

"A long time coming," Shawn said.

A portly man with curly red hair, dressed in a red and green plaid kilt, stood at the top of the steps. The air filled with the sounds of his bagpipe as he played a slow version of *Isn't She Lovely?* by Stevie Wonder. Aleesha made her way down the aisle, grinning as though this was her special day. Natasha followed her while darting her eyes across the crowd. They both held bouquets of violets.

The bagpiper finished the song. Then two more bagpipers dressed in matching kilts stepped over to join the first one. Together, they played Amazing Grace. The chords were deep and stirring.

Violet appeared, looking stunning in an elegant, flowing white dress. She caught Shawn's eyes and didn't look away. Shawn had never seen her look more ravishing. His mind filled up with her loveliness.

Violet's eyes looked like jewels set against her glowing, joyful face.

Shawn could feel his heart swell as a lightness filled his chest. His eyes sparkled and gleamed as she approached. Everything went silent around him. It felt like it was just the two of them. He fought to keep the tears in, but one slipped through.

Violet glided down the aisle and walked up the steps to the platform. She took Shawn's hands in hers. They turned to face each other as the pastor spoke. "We are gathered here today in the sight of God and these witnesses to join together Violet and Shawn."

"Olivia. It's Olivia," she said. Her face bloomed with a radiant smile. Shawn beamed his own look of delight.

"Olivia and Shawn," the pastor said, "to celebrate the uniting of their hearts and lives."

Shawn focused on Olivia's white dress as the pastor spoke. The milky color pulsated with life and blended with the sounds of the vibrant flowers surrounding them to create a beautiful melody in his mind. A tear slipped down his cheek.

Before they knew it, Shawn and Olivia were gazing deep into each other's eyes as they said, "I do."

"What symbol do you bring as a pledge of the sincerity of your vows?" the pastor asked.

"A ring," Shawn said. Olivia looked at Colin for the rings, but he grinned and didn't move. Instead, Ruth stood up in the front row, walked up the steps, and handed Shawn her wedding rings.

"Thank you," Olivia whispered to her. Ruth gave her a long hug before she took her seat.

Finally, the moment arrived. "Ladies and gentlemen," the pastor said, "may I present to you, Mr. and Mrs. Shawn and Olivia Lambent." The crowd exploded with applause. Shawn leaned forward and kissed Olivia. It was a tender, romantic kiss that filled his mouth with sweet softness and felt electrifying. As the crowd applauded, the Manhattan skyline illuminated all around them with its magnificent colors and sounds.

# MAKE A DIFFERENCE

Thank you for reading *The Sound of Violet*. If you enjoyed the story, would you please leave a review at your favorite retailer and recommend it to a friend? I hope you'll check out our movie as well.

A portion of sales from this novel are donated to fight human trafficking. If you or someone you know is caught in trafficking or you suspect human trafficking, call 1-888-373-7888 or text "help" to BeFree (233733). The toll-free hotline is available to answer calls from anywhere in the United States, 24 hours a day in more than 200 languages.

For additional resources to fight human trafficking or information about autism, visit TheSoundOfViolet.com.

Together, we can make a difference.

All the best,

Allen Wolf

# ABOUT ALLEN WOLF

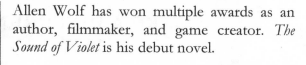

Allen Wolf has won multiple awards as an author, filmmaker, and game creator. *The Sound of Violet* is his debut novel.

As a filmmaker, he wrote, directed, and produced the movie version of *The Sound of Violet*, based on this novel. Allen's first feature film, *In My Sleep*, was released worldwide and won multiple film festival awards.

Allen is also the host of the popular Navigating Hollywood podcast where he interviews entertainment professionals about their careers and how they thrive in Hollywood.

Allen has won 39 awards for the games he created, including *You're Pulling My Leg!*, *You're Pulling My Leg! Junior*, *Slap Wacky*, *JabberJot*, and *Pet Detectives*. These games have brought smiles to hundreds of thousands of people around the world. Allen's *You're Pulling My Leg!* game makes an appearance in *The Sound of Violet* as well as *In My Sleep*.

Allen graduated from New York University's film school, where his senior thesis film, *Harlem Grace*, won multiple festival awards and was a finalist for the *Student Academy Awards*.

Allen married his Persian princess, and they are raising their daughter and son in Los Angeles. He enjoys traveling around the world and hearing people's life stories. He also cherishes playing games with his family, tasting chocolate, and Disneyland.

Connect with Allen:

AllenWolf.com
TheSoundOfViolet.com

 @theAllenWolf

# MOVIE STILLS

"We need to get you on a second date."
Left to right: Jan D'Arcy as Ruth, Cason Thomas as Shawn

"Find a way to reward this beauty."
Left to right: Tyler Roy Roberts as Jake, Cason Thomas as Shawn

"What do you do to earn that much?"
Left to right: Cora Cleary as Violet, Cason Thomas as Shawn

# MOVIE STILLS

"Oh, you want the girlfriend experience?"
Left to right: Cora Cleary as Violet, Cason Thomas as Shawn

"So this is an audition?"
Left to right: Cora Cleary as Violet, Cason Thomas as Shawn

"I'm going to create a cereal called 'Enemies' so people can eat them for breakfast."
Left to right: Cora Cleary as Violet, Cason Thomas as Shawn

# MOVIE STILLS

"Productive night, sweetie?"
Left to right: Michael E. Bell as Anton, Cora Cleary as Violet

"I want to see you again."
Left to right: Cason Thomas as Shawn, Kaelon Christopher as Colin, Cora Cleary as Violet

"You know, sometimes we need a little encouragement, so we don't give up on love."
Left to right: Jan D'Arcy as Ruth, Cason Thomas as Shawn

# MOVIE STILLS

"That's the best I can do."
Left to right: Cason Thomas as Shawn, Cora Cleary as Violet

"Wish I had someone to go for a walk with me when I get off at five."
Left to right: Malcolm J. West as Douglas, Jan D'Arcy as Ruth

Left to right: Cason Thomas as Shawn, Cora Cleary as Violet

# BEHIND THE SCENES OF THE MOVIE

Left to right: Cora Cleary as Violet, Cason Thomas as Shawn

Left to right: Cora Cleary as Violet, Cason Thomas as Shawn with Writer, Director, Producer Allen Wolf

Filming the opening scenes at Gas Works Park in Seattle.

# BEHIND THE SCENES OF THE MOVIE

Writer, Director, Producer Allen Wolf shares the director's seat with his daughter.

Left to right: Cora Cleary as Violet, Cason Thomas as Shawn

The crew prepares to film a scene with actor Cason Thomas.

# BEHIND THE SCENES OF THE MOVIE

Filming the restaurant scene.

The cast and crew watches playback of one of the scenes.

Director of Photography Chris Taylor (left) films Cora Cleary and Cason Thomas while Allen Wolf directs.

# BEHIND THE SCENES OF THE MOVIE

Enthusiastic extras prepare to film an important scene.

Left to right: Michael E. Bell as Anton with Writer, Director, Producer Allen Wolf.

Composer Conrad Pope conducts the orchestra while recording the score for *The Sound of Violet*.

# BOOK CLUB DISCUSSION QUESTIONS

1. What were your favorite and least favorite parts of the story?
2. How did the book make you feel?
3. How did the story impact how you view autism?
4. How did your view of Shawn change throughout the book?
5. How did the story impact how you view trafficking?
6. How did your view of Violet change throughout the book?
7. Which characters did you like the most and least?
8. What surprised you about the story?
9. How were you able to relate to any of the character's journeys?
10. How would you describe the spiritual journeys of the characters? How would you describe your own?
11. What did you think about the ending?
12. What were your biggest takeaways from the book?
13. If you continued the storyline, what would you want to happen next?

# AFTER WATCHING THE MOVIE:

1. What did you like best and least about the movie?
2. What differences did you notice between the book and film?
3. How did the movie compare to what you envisioned while reading the book?
4. What parts of the film stood out to you most?
5. What did you like about the movie that wasn't part of the book?
6. What moments did you prefer from the book rather than the film?
7. How would you describe the spiritual journeys of the characters? How would you describe your own?
8. How did the movie make you feel?
9. How did the film impact your perspective on trafficking and autism?
10. If you created the sequel to the movie, how would you continue the story?

# MOVIES FROM ALLEN WOLF

Experience *The Sound of Violet* come to life in the motion picture version of the novel that was written, directed, and produced by author Allen Wolf.

Discover more about the movie at TheSoundOfViolet.com.

"A very sweet and endearing romantic comedy, with an excellent relationship between Violet and Shawn at the center."
*- The Black List*

"A rewardingly nuanced, three-dimensional, and charming – if unconventional – love story. Strong character voices define the entirety of the plot, while the genuine chemistry between the central roles creates a natural, seemingly effortless appeal within both their relationships and their perspectives in broader terms. Superb characters, strong dialogue, and a polished overall execution wind up rendering a finished product that seems in many ways both moving and entertaining."
*- Script Shark*

"*The Sound of Violet* is a fluently written romantic comedy that both acknowledges and deviates from the conventions in a sparky, original manner. While this set up might seem wildly implausible at first glance, it's established in a very organic way, with warmth, intelligence and wit – three qualities that characterize the rest of the screenplay. Overall, this screenplay achieves the rare feat of being both funny and romantic, delivering an emotionally satisfying ending to Violet and Shawn's misadventures, without patronizing the audience."
*- BlueCat Screenplay Competition*

# MOVIES FROM ALLEN WOLF

Allen Wolf wrote, directed and produced the psychological thriller, *In My Sleep*, which won multiple festival awards including *Best Picture* and the *Audience Award*. See more at MorningStarPictures.com.

---

"Savvy Entertainment. Filmmaker Allen Wolf torques this high-concept premise to darkest dimension. Narratively, *In My Sleep* never rests, a credit to the tight, psychologically astute pacing of filmmaker Wolf."

*- The Hollywood Reporter*

"Genuinely suspenseful moments."

*- New York Magazine*

"*In My Sleep* is a brilliantly written thriller that genuinely keeps one guessing throughout the movie. The pacing is superb and the performances topnotch. Allen Wolf has created a very well made thriller."

*- Movie Guide*

---

# MOVIES FROM ALLEN WOLF

Allen Wolf wrote, directed and produced the drama short *Harlem Grace* that has won multiple awards. This true story chronicles the amazing impact of one dedicated individual on the lives of homeless men after he graduates from Harvard Law School and decides to move to Harlem to start a homeless shelter.

*Harlem Grace* teaches powerful lessons about trust, grace, perseverance, and the power of redemption.

See more about *Harlem Grace* at MorningStarPictures.com.

---

"Crisply acted and directed, *Harlem Grace* is an uplifting, redemptive film. Harlem Grace will inspire and edify the entire family and cheer and encourage moral Americans that godly diligence and hard work can transform otherwise hopeless people's lives."　　　*– Movie Guide*

"A film as polished and straightforward as its well-groomed and self-assured subject, Joe Holland. Wolf's real achievement is not unlike his film's hero: his film dares to propose that faith and hard work can solve problems and save lives."　　　*– Dayton Daily News*

"Wolf has accomplished a fare artistic feat. Allen Wolf manages to put a human face on a dehumanizing problem. An engrossing spectacle, rich in subtlety, political inference and social commentary. Totally engages its viewers. Wolf has accomplished a rare artistic feat. The viewer sees the power in establishing meaningful human relationships even where there exist seemingly unfathomable social distance in class, education, and experience."　　　*– Amsterdam News*

---

# GAMES FROM ALLEN WOLF

You'll laugh out loud as you and your friends try to fool each other with hilarious stories about your lives while your play the original *You're Pulling My Leg!* game for Adults and Teens.

Think you know your friends? How well do they know you? Bluff other players but don't let them fool you. Score enough points, and you win! Winner of 8 Awards.

See more at MorningStarGames.com.

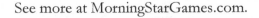

"Great for new friends. This game makes a terrific icebreaker and getting-to-know-you activity."       — *Real Simple Magazine*

"If you're looking for a party game, this is the best you can find."
                                                              — *The Dice Tower*

"Simple, easy, and fun to play. Great thought-provoking questions. Never became boring. Great group activity for teenagers and adults. Everyone had a good time."       — *iParenting Media Awards*

"Great family, dating, group or party game. Helps you get to know one another better and makes for a lot of laughing. The more you play the more creative your answers will become."       — *Family Games Review*

# GAMES FROM ALLEN WOLF

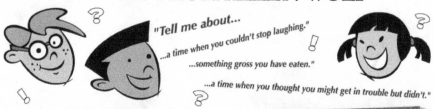

Have you ever eaten five pizzas? Gotten gum stuck in your hair? Surprised a friend?

In this hilarious game for families and kids ages 9+, your friends and family try to bluff each other with your answers to questions like these while you play *You're Pulling My Leg! Junior.*

Winner of 7 Awards!

See more at MorningStarGames.com.

---

"The kids got a big kick out of this game and could not stop laughing."
*- Parent to Parent*

"Teaches while challenging children to understand what makes an interesting, compelling and believable story. Knowing your audience, playing to that audience and selling your ideas are some pretty heavy things to find in a simple game, but that is just what testers reported witnessing in their children as they played this game over and over. Along the way you'll be surprised how much you learn either about your own kids or about others." *- The National Parenting Center*

"This is pure fun! We loved this game. It made us laugh hysterically. Encourages the players to interact and gives them a chance to learn about each other." *- iParenting Media Awards*

---

# GAMES FROM ALLEN WOLF

Discover the world of laugh-out-loud storymaking! Race against the timer to create stories using pictures, words, and a theme that change for each round.

You'll laugh hysterically when you hear the stories your friends and family create. *JabberJot* will inspire your imagination!

Winner of 11 Awards!

See more at MorningStarGames.com.

"One of the most imaginative games we have ever seen. Requires players to bring a sense of fun, silliness and creativity to the table. Perfect for large groups at a party, or for a quiet family game night with as few as four players, *JabberJot* keeps the action moving and the wild storylines flowing. You will laugh, groan and smile as you Jabber and Jot."                                  *- The National Parenting Center*

"This game will help your child improve vocabulary and creative writing skills. Turn visual images and words into stories while engaging in endless imagination."                                  *- Dr. Toy*

"This is a great party game. Fun and educational too."
*- iParenting Media Awards*

# GAMES FROM ALLEN WOLF

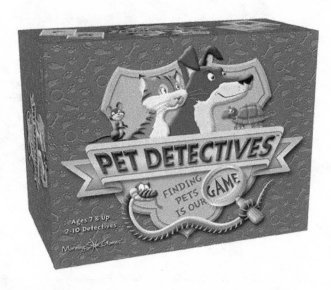

Pets have gone missing and it's up to you to find them! *Pet Detectives* puts kids and families on the path to finding their fun, furry friends in order to become the best pet detective in town.

Winner of 7 Awards! See more at MorningStarGames.com.

---

"Results in a completely entertaining evening that you can play with your kids. The names of the animal characters will launch peals of laughter."
- The National Parenting Center

"It's entertaining and fun. Incorporates positive values and allows the whole family to play together."
- Dr. Toy

"Our test family had a blast playing Pet Detectives. In fact, our young players wanted to play over and over again. Kids will love the adorable pictures of animals, and parents will love that their kids strengthen counting and memory skills."
- Parent Zone

---